'Cured of wh

'Would you bel
challenged. 'Or
behind?'

'Not for an instant,' she retorted. 'I imagine you're far too strong a character to let an irrational emotion like love cause you a moment's angst.'

'Speaking from experience, Dr Cochrane?' he countered, surprised that so attractive a woman would speak so slightingly of love.

'Not of love,' she assured him. 'Lust maybe, but so long ago any angst that might have existed is well and truly forgotten.'

'You don't class lust as an irrational emotion?'

'I class lust as over-active hormones,' Sally said firmly. 'Purely physiological. Now, shall we get back to splitting the team?'

'Pre-empting a decision?' Grant teased.

'Merely smoothing the way for a possible transition,' she said, but the gold lights danced in her eyes and he couldn't help but smile.

Purely physiological, he reminded himself!

THE AUSTRALIAN DOCTORS

Identical twins, identically single—they're about to learn there's more to life than medicine!

Identical twins Tom and Grant Hudson have had their fair share of women problems but they're about to be discovered by two women who will change their lives and their outlook on love and marriage.

In *Claimed: One Wife* neurosurgeon Grant Hudson is against fraternisation amongst his medical team.
He has his reasons; they're hidden in his past.
But Dr Sally Cochrane is enough to make him break all his own rules. A man can only resist so much!

CLAIMED:
ONE WIFE

BY
MEREDITH WEBBER

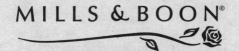

MILLS & BOON®

DID YOU PURCHASE THIS BOOK WITHOUT A COVER?

If you did, you should be aware it is **stolen property** as it was reported *unsold and destroyed* by a retailer. Neither the author nor the publisher has received any payment for this book.

All the characters in this book have no existence outside the imagination of the author, and have no relation whatsoever to anyone bearing the same name or names. They are not even distantly inspired by any individual known or unknown to the author, and all the incidents are pure invention.

All Rights Reserved including the right of reproduction in whole or in part in any form. This edition is published by arrangement with Harlequin Enterprises II B.V. The text of this publication or any part thereof may not be reproduced or transmitted in any form or by any means, electronic or mechanical, including photocopying, recording, storage in an information retrieval system, or otherwise, without the written permission of the publisher.

This book is sold subject to the condition that it shall not, by way of trade or otherwise, be lent, resold, hired out or otherwise circulated without the prior consent of the publisher in any form of binding or cover other than that in which it is published and without a similar condition including this condition being imposed on the subsequent purchaser.

MILLS & BOON and MILLS & BOON with the Rose Device are registered trademarks of the publisher.

First published in Great Britain 2001
Harlequin Mills & Boon Limited,
Eton House, 18-24 Paradise Road, Richmond, Surrey TW9 1SR

© Meredith Webber 2001

ISBN 0 263 82661 9

Set in Times Roman 10¼ on 11½ pt.
03-0501-52053

Printed and bound in Spain
by Litografia Rosés, S.A., Barcelona

CHAPTER ONE

THIS mixed-sex changing room was the most ridiculous thing he'd ever encountered, Grant Hudson decided, grabbing surgical pyjamas out of the box labelled LARGE and heading for the furthest corner of the room. Not that he had anything against small, neat female bodies clad in sensible white cotton underwear. It was just that he found them distracting in a work environment.

He put the pyjamas down on the bench and took off his tie, which reminded him of the dinner date he was missing, peeled off his shirt and hung it on a hanger. Tried focussing on work rather than Jocelyn.

Or Tom.

Or the small, neat female body clad in sensible white cotton underwear!

It was the *theory* behind the mixed dressing room experiment that rankled. The idea that there'd be a cross-fertilisation of ideas as surgeons chatted with other surgeons while they changed. This room was designated for use by teams operating in Theatres Five and Six, which meant that most mornings, prior to the start of regular surgical shifts, there could be a dozen men and women—orthopods, neurologists, general surgeons and medical students—all stripping down to their underwear.

In practice, the staff he'd encountered in here since his arrival at the hospital a little over a week ago changed in almost total silence. After all, it was hard to conduct a conversation with an underwear-clad female colleague, trying all the time to ensure your eyes were on her face, while wondering if your own boxer shorts might be gaping open at an inappropriate place.

Tonight the room seemed cavernous as well as quiet. A couple of surgeons he didn't know were dressing, and Sally Cochrane, his fourth-year neurosurgery resident—she of the neat body—was doing her own thing down near the door.

Grant took off his shoes, and eased his trousers down over his hips. Then, sitting on the bench so any inadvertent gaping would go unnoticed, he whipped them off and drew on the bottom half of his surgical suit, leaving the waist tie loose while he got into the top.

The top felt tight and the recurrent regret that surgical clothing was rarely made in a size large enough to accommodate his height and bulk had barely flashed through his head when he heard his resident's complaint.

'OK. Who swapped the labels on the boxes? I suppose you think this is funny!'

She stomped up the narrow room, her arms spread wide, a suit three sizes too big engulfing her compact body, making her look like a half-deflated balloon.

Then she caught sight of him and began to laugh. To *point* and laugh. Rich, earthy laughter which seemed inappropriate coming from such a small, dainty woman.

'Oh, dear, I'm sorry,' she gasped. 'But you look so funny. I know I must, too. It's ridiculous, but—oh…'

She gave way to the laughter again, while Grant stood up very slowly because he feared what he would see, then held his own arms wide and looked down at his legs.

Yep! The trousers ended mid-calf, the sleeves mid-forearm.

He scowled at the laughing female, then at the staff who were hurriedly exiting the room, their shoulders shaking as if they, too, found the situation hilarious.

'We've a patient waiting, Dr Cochrane,' he said, stripping

off the too-small top then realising he'd have to ask her where the 'large' box was.

She controlled herself long enough to pull off her top as well, again revealing the neat white cotton bra. Very white against her tanned skin. When did she have time to sunbathe? And would she tan so deeply if she used UV protection?

Better to feel righteous about her likely neglect of health considerations than wonder if the tan went all over her neatly packaged torso.

'Here, have this one,' she said, casually handing him the garment she'd shed.

Pleased to have a diversion, he took it and pulled it on, then immediately regretted that decision. The faint perfume of her body, a hint of flowery sweetness that sometimes lingered in his office after a team meeting, rose from the warmed material.

Now he'd have it in his nostrils right through the operation.

Not that she seemed fazed by any lingering body odour he might have left in his top, for she'd scooped it up off the bench and put it on before bending to take off the too-large trousers and pass them to him.

'We could both have taken new sets,' he pointed out, stiffly formal as the sight of slim brown legs stretching below the soft aqua of their theatre garb had his body reacting in a most inappropriate manner.

'I suppose we could, but if the boxes are all mixed up, we might have tried on four pairs before we found the right fit. At least I knew you had my size.'

She gave another chuckle, then, perhaps realising he wasn't sharing her mirth, smothered it and turned away, giving him a rear view of her neat backside as she bent to put first one foot, then the other, into the loose trousers.

Sally pulled the drawstring tight and tied it at her waist as she walked away. Her insides were shaking with tension, but there'd been no way she was going to be reduced to mush by one of Grant Hudson's scowls.

OK, so he didn't see the funny side of her in swamping garments and himself in the too-small set, but he didn't have to go all cold and formal.

He could at least have smiled.

If he could produce such an expression.

An image of his face presented itself in her head. Dark hair, cut crisply short, lightly tanned skin, vivid blue eyes looking sternly down at her from behind the clear-lensed glasses he wore to operate.

She banished the image, suspicious of eyes with such mesmeric power. Suspicious of her own reaction to a man who obviously held her in disdain.

Thought about smiles instead.

Perhaps he lacked the necessary muscles to pull his lips into the smiling position. Perhaps she could knock him out one day and do an exploratory investigation of his cranial nerves to see if something was missing. Limiting his ability to crack a grin.

But the thought of carving into Grant Hudson's firm skin, and seeing the bones that gave his face such a strong structure, lessened the appeal of the idea.

'Are you ready, Doctor?'

The sound of his voice, quietly resonant, brought Sally out of her daydreams. She bit back the 'call me Sally' retort she'd made the first dozen times he'd called her 'Doctor', and nodded, meekly following him out of the changing room towards the scrub room.

Then trod on his slippers and ran into his back when he stopped suddenly.

He untangled himself, and bent to adjust the loose slipper. Scowled again. She could read the 'have you always been this clumsy?' question in his eyes.

She was about to apologise when a new voice chipped in.

'Tripping over yourself as usual, Sal?'

Sally found it was her turn to scowl.

Daniel Denton, the neuro registrar, wasn't her favourite person. But these days, the way he pandered to the new boss not only irritated her but made her feel uncomfortable. His presence here tonight was an example of this behaviour. He wasn't on duty or on call, but wherever the new neurosurgery head was, Daniel wouldn't be far away.

'I did not trip over!' she informed him, and was about to add that eight years of ballet lessons had actually left her quite light on her feet, but Daniel, having derived whatever satisfaction he enjoyed from needling her, had turned his attention to their department head.

'I wondered if I could have a moment before you start,' Daniel continued, all charm and false humility as he faced their new master. 'Perhaps while Sal sets up?'

He moved his head to indicate the changing room she and Grant had just vacated, and, instead of reminding Daniel that patients came first, Grant Hudson simply turned to Sally, said, 'We'll need a laminectomy frame,' then followed Daniel back into the changing room.

Sally walked through to the theatre and felt her ill humour melt away when she saw Sam Abbot there.

'I thought you'd left us for the joys of ICU,' she said to the nurse.

'I'm floating between ICU and Theatre, and circulating here tonight. Jackie Wells is scrubbing,' Sam explained. 'Do you need anything?'

'Laminectomy frame. You know the contraption? And extra sterile drapes to go over it.'

She worked with Sam and the anaesthetist, Harry Strutt, to set it up and lift the patient onto it, then headed to the scrub room.

'You're scrubbing very forcefully this evening,' Jackie remarked, coming in to help Sally gown up. 'Anything upsetting you?'

'Just men in general, and a couple in particular,' Sally told her, treating her forearms to the brush attack. 'It's bad enough to have that know-all, smarmy, toad-eating registrar directly over me, but, to make matters worse, the new boss is a cranky, stiff-necked bear of a man who—'

A rumble of male conversation told her the door had swung open and she swallowed the rest of the sentence, praying the bear wouldn't recognise himself from her description.

'Shove over, Sal,' Daniel said, coming to stand too close to her at the next basin.

'Don't call me Sal,' she snapped at him, then she took the paper towels Jackie was offering and, keeping her arms above waist height, carefully dried her fingers.

She moved away from the basins, letting Jackie help to gown and glove her, tucking the ends of the gown sleeves into the gloves.

Then, without further comment, she scurried back into the theatre.

She stood silently awaiting orders as the new boss strode in and introduced himself. Daniel hovered sycophantically behind him and earned a glare from Sally for simply being alive.

Not a good way to begin an emergency operation.

And it had only got worse! Sam, usually one of the best theatre nurses, had dropped something which had clanged so loudly in the unnatural silence it had jarred against Sally's nerves. Grant Hudson had received a phone call which had obviously upset him, if the expression in his cool blue eyes had been any guide. Daniel had aggravated her to such an extent she'd been tempted to tattoo him with the electrocautery pen.

Grant, once he'd informed her she was doing the job, had stayed long enough to make her feel uncomfortable, although he'd been more helpful than intrusive. And, to be honest, she'd appreciated his working with her, treating her as an equal rather than as a student. Daniel had also assisted, and the big boss's consideration and lack of comment had highlighted Daniel's aggravating habit of reminding her of every cut, scoop or chip she had to make.

In the end it had been Grant Hudson who'd suggested she was managing quite well without Daniel's interference, and she'd shot him a grateful glance.

Once the clot they'd been seeking had been removed and the damaged vessel that had caused it repaired, Grant Hudson had departed, having taken so little part in the operation she wondered if he'd used it as a test of some kind for her. Would he do the same with the others on the neuro team?

Haunt their nights on duty with his presence?

She worked with Daniel now, drawing the layers of the wound together, closing it neatly and efficiently. There was a definite easing of the tension in the room, but all the 'end of operation' questions had come to torment her. Had they got it soon enough? Made sure there wouldn't be a re-bleed? Was there any other damage to his body which might affect the patient's recovery? Something the ER team had missed as they worried about his paralysis?

'Well, that's the quietest operation I've been part of for a long time,' Jackie said, as Sally stepped back to allow Daniel to finish the closing.

'Might be a sign of things to come,' Sally replied, rolling her shoulders to ease the pain of too many hours' tense concentration. 'He's hardly the cheeriest soul I've ever met.'

'That could be something to do with him hearing your comment,' Daniel told her, his voice soft with malice. 'The bit about the stiff-necked, cranky bear.'

Sally hid a groan, refusing to give Daniel the satisfaction of knowing he'd scored.

'Or something to do with the woman who phoned. Maybe

he stood her up to be in on this op,' Helen, Harry's anaesthetic nurse, said. 'She sounded really cheesed off.'

'Private phone calls during an operation? Wasn't that one of the list of things he decreed unprofessional?'

Sally turned to Daniel, who would be the only other person in the room who'd seen the briefing notes Grant Hudson had handed out when he'd taken over as head of the neurosurgery department the previous week.

Daniel was supervising the intern who was stitching up the wound, and pretended this task was taking all of his attention. He wasn't going to risk some chance remark being overheard, or perhaps repeated in the boss's hearing.

'But most of the senior surgeons bring in pagers and mobile phones, especially at night when there's no theatre secretary to take messages,' Helen pointed out. 'They just dump them under the anaesthetist's trolley and expect me to answer for them. And I'm sure half the calls aren't relevant to work.'

'New brooms,' Harry said. 'See it all the time. New department heads like to feel they've got the place structured their way. We had a head of anaesthetics one time who felt we should work different rotations. Didn't bother to enquire why I'd been on call or on duty at night for fifteen years. I had a devil of a job sorting things out.'

'How is Marion?' Sally asked him, thinking of Harry's wife, who'd developed Parkinson's disease fifteen years earlier. Harry liked to be at home with her during the day, sleeping when she slept or when a paid carer was present. He was freed up at night by his daughter who still lived at home.

'The new tablets are good. Take about half an hour to work, but once she's taken one she can hold a pencil. She can do a crossword even if she can't write a letter.'

Sally smiled at the anaesthetist, but her thoughts were on his wife, who, from all accounts, had been a top surgeon until the disease had caused uncontrollable tremors in her hands. Parkinson's was one of many areas of neurosurgery she could opt to pursue. The early operations for it had been too extreme, but some new methods were being trialled...

'We're all done here if you want to dress it,' Daniel said, and Sally put off thinking about the future to concentrate on the present. She moved back towards the table, supervising the dressing of the wound, wondering again how well the patient would be when he woke up.

'He's all yours,' she told the anaesthetist, thankfully handing over the responsibility for their patient.

But the unusual silence in the theatre, the lack of jokes and ribald comments, had added to the tension, so she could feel her bones, tugged and pulled by strung-out tendons, aching for relief.

However, it would all have been worthwhile if their patient came out of it with movement in his limbs.

'No response to stimuli in his hands or feet,' the nurse who was specialling the patient in the ICU told Sally when she dragged her still-tired body on duty early next morning. Three hours' sleep was never enough, and her mind felt doughy and drugged.

She surveyed her slumbering patient.

'Hello, Craig,' she said, hoping the use of his name might make him more alert.

To her surprise, he opened his eyes and looked at her.

'I'm Sally Cochrane, your surgeon. We've removed a blood clot from your spine. That's what was causing the paralysis. Because of the pressure, it may be a while before you regain all feeling, but Dr Hudson, the head of the department, is confident you'll make a full recovery.'

'Did I say that?' a quiet voice murmured in her ear, and she spun around to see the doctor in question directly behind her. And although she knew he'd had as little sleep as she'd had—possibly less as the chart showed he'd seen Craig after he was settled in the ICU—he looked as alert, fresh and well groomed as he always did.

With her usually shiny dark hair still flat and lifeless from the theatre cap, she probably looked as she felt, like something the cat had dragged in.

Not that it should matter, should it?

'You implied it,' she told him in a grim undertone, too low for the patient to hear. 'And how do you creep up on people like that? Special rubber-soled shoes?'

He didn't bother to answer, merely stepping forward and introducing himself to the man, and reiterating Sally's views that recovery, while slow, would be fairly certain.

'Can you be confident he'll recover movement when we don't know how the spinal cord has been affected by the insult of the clot?' she asked as they left the room. Her irritation had dissolved as she'd watched Grant Hudson in action, reassuring an understandably fearful patient, so it was a natural question to ask as they left the room together.

Grant nodded, confidently, and the smile she'd doubted he could summon appeared very briefly.

'Always take into account the other indicators. His general health, for one thing. Craig's a lifesaver. He's on the beach most weekends. Swims, trains. He's fit as a Mallee bull.'

'Fit as a Mallee bull,' Sally repeated, turning to look into eyes that seemed bluer without the glasses he wore for surgery. 'My father used to say that.'

For the first time she felt a slight quiver of empathy with the autocratic man fate had decreed should be her boss.

Well, she hoped it was only empathy!

Grant heard his senior resident repeat the silly metaphor and imagined a softness in her tone. Not that there would be anything soft about Sally Cochrane. It was hard for anyone to get onto one of the specialist surgical programmes, but for women it was doubly difficult. Although fifty per cent of medical students were females, few made it to the upper echelons of power. The Council of the College of Surgeons was male dominated, as was the executive of the Neurological Surgeons Association. And the Surgical Board and Court of Examiners who set the oral and written neurosurgery examinations and assessed the trainees were all men.

So far! he reminded himself grimly. Although it was only a matter of time…

He shut away the memories that had briefly flashed into his head and considered Sally Cochrane once again.

To do as well as she had done, she must be far tougher than her delicately put-together frame and pretty face suggested.

And as he studied the pretty face in question, or what he could see of it without making his scrutiny obvious, he found some of the tension of the last few days—a combination of a new job and a lost brother, to say nothing of a persistent headache and the onset of arthritis in his left ankle—easing out of his nerves.

Though where the hell *was* Tom? How could he just disappear on the road between Sydney and Brisbane?

'How soon will we know?'

Dark brown eyes, lit by tiny flashes of gold, looked up at him as she asked a question. It took him a moment to realise the conversation had swung back to their patient's progress. No personal byplay for Sally Cochrane! No, sir, this was one member of his team who had no intention of sweet-talking the boss!

'Maybe days, maybe months,' he told her, reminding himself it was how he liked to work. Professionally close to his colleagues, but personally keeping them at arm's length. His own experience with Erica had left him hurting, then the disaster with the two young residents a few years later had reinforced his determination to keep personal and professional life separate. Less distracting, and better for all concerned.

'If it stretches to months I'll get the heebie-jeebies,' she said, and again the gold-lit eyes scanned his face. 'Doesn't your worry factor balloon out of all control when it takes longer than it reasonably or logically should for improvement to reveal itself?'

'Heebie-jeebies.' He found himself smiling in spite of his determination to remain aloof. 'My turn to be surprised by an expression. I haven't heard it since I was a kid. But it perfectly describes the uncertainty.'

He stopped smiling so she didn't get any ideas, and added, 'When that happens I remind myself we haven't made anything worse. I mean, he'd have been paralysed for life if we'd left the clot. At least, by operating, we've given him a chance.'

'A chance!' she repeated quietly. 'It's not like other surgery, is it? We open up bits of people that should never be disturbed, and it's only ever giving them a chance. No certain outcome, in the way removing an appendix will stop the pain.'

'But could cause peritonitis,' he countered. 'While joint replacements can leave patients far worse off if infection sets in. There are no guarantees in any of our specialties so don't get maudlin on me, Dr Cochrane. I'm into positive thinking as far as all the patients under my care are concerned.'

'Even the pain patients?' she asked, and he realised that, far from being maudlin, she was now teasing him. 'Positive relief?'

He sighed.

'Eighty-five per cent of all neuro patients are seeking relief from pain,' he reminded her. 'And more than half of them we can help.' He caught the twitch of her very shapely lips as she hid a smile. Then, annoyed with himself for being distracted, he said sternly, 'Mrs Franklin is an exception, I'll admit, but her pain is genuine to her.'

'Hot horses' hooves thundering down her spine? Gnomes

pressing flaming needles into her flesh?' Sally Cochrane murmured, the smile no longer hidden and the gold in her eyes gleaming with delight.

'Patients with psychosomatic pain do tend towards more colourful descriptions,' he agreed, then he shrugged, determined to distance himself again. 'But we can't just turn them away. We have to try to alleviate it.'

They walked out of the ICU together, towards the lifts which would take them up to the neurosurgery ward where previously treated patients would be awaiting their morning visit.

'Are you going to try an implanted stimulator on her?' Sally asked as they crowded into the lift.

'It's about all that's left,' he admitted. 'If she can get some relief from it, she can then go to detox and be taken slowly off the morphine.'

He sighed, rejecting a spurt of anger with the patient's previous doctor who'd continued the pain relief without considering other options. After all, the implanting of an electrode in the spine was relatively new and the physician who'd been treating Mrs Franklin had been a family friend and unwilling to risk her ire by cutting back on her drugs.

Daniel joined them when they reached the ward, with young Paul Adams, an intern on a short rotation to Neurosurgery which was offered as an adjunct to the surgical rotation. The charge nurse and a group of eight students made up the crew who'd be doing the formal round.

Grant nodded his head towards the tearoom and they all crowded in. Daniel produced the patient cards and, as he read out a name, Sally outlined the patient's problem or problems then deferred to the boss for his input.

He spoke well, she decided. Putting facts to the students in clear, succinct terms which would make them easy to absorb. That was if they weren't thinking about the little smile lines fanning out from his eyes when he half smiled.

Unlikely, as they were all young men! She really had to get
her act together here. Apart from the fact Grant Hudson
wasn't interested in her—*and* wasn't likely to be, given his
stand on intra-team relationships—romance and study didn't
mix, remember.

'"Millie Franklin",' Daniel read. '"Fifty-seven, married.
Ten year history of extreme back pain."'

Sally forgot smile lines and took over, professionally de-
scribing the laminectomies Mrs Franklin had undergone under other specialists.

'In many cases, the removal of ruptured discs and the fus-
ing of the spine provides relief for back pain-sufferers.' Grant
Hudson expanded on the subject. 'However, this hasn't
worked for Mrs Franklin and this time she's in to have an
electrode implanted in her spine. The operation is done under
anaesthetic.'

He went on to explain exactly how the tiny wire would be
inserted into her spine and over the spinal cord. Sally, relieved from speaking duties, relaxed as she listened to the
rise and fall of his voice. The dark notes in it were soft and
mellow, almost seductive…

'Are you still with us, Dr Cochrane?'

She shook herself awake.

'I was asking you to explain what happens next.'

Next?

She caught sight of Daniel's smirk, then fortunately saw
the slight movement of Paul's fingers.

'We attach the electrode to a control box and the patient
is given the controls so he or she can experiment with different levels of stimulation.'

'Thank you, Dr Cochrane, and Dr Adams for the prompt,'
Grant said smoothly. 'And then?' he looked at Sally again.

'Once we know what stimulation helps we take the patient
back to Theatre and insert a radio receiver to the electrode
and pack the lot under the skin to keep it sterile. The patient

wears a transmitter on his or her waist, or carries it in some other way, and can send the messages to the electrode which produces a buzzing sensation.'

Grant nodded. 'The theory is it gates the pain—provides a distraction that stops the pain messages getting through to the brain.'

He turned to ask the students if they had any questions.

Naturally they did, and Sally had to hide a sigh. Both Daniel and Ted, the previous head of the neurology department, hated student rounds and got through them with a minimum of fuss and a maximum of disdain for the underlings.

She disapproved of this approach and tried to make it up to the students at other times, but surely there was a happy medium somewhere between their way and Grant Hudson's.

She must have sighed again, for the man in question fixed her with a steely glare.

'Are we keeping you from something, Dr Cochrane?'

Not that he could have expected a reply, for he was on his feet, heading for the door, the students trailing in his wake.

'You'll have to do more than flash a pretty smile to impress this fellow,' Daniel said, falling in behind and walking, too close, beside her.

'If you're implying what I think you're implying, I could sue you!' she snapped, stepping sideways to avoid the proximity.

Daniel laughed.

'You're telling me you didn't go running to Ted when I made a pass at you?'

The question was so surprising, that Sally stopped dead.

'Running to Ted? To tell him you'd a made a pass? You've got to be joking!'

But a hardness in Daniel's eyes suggested he wasn't, and Sally wondered if the aggravation she put up with from him didn't stem entirely from her refusal to join his 'hospital harem'.

'Since Ted had trouble seeing the nose on the front of his face, I doubt he noticed anything himself, Sal,' Daniel murmured.

Sally felt her spine stiffen, and tiredness overcame the restraint she usually employed in his presence.

'Don't call me Sal!' she growled at him. 'You know damn well how much I hate it!'

'When you're ready, Dr Cochrane.'

Grant's voice froze her blood.

She nodded, and followed the crew into the ward, battling mortification now, as well as anger. But soon the joy of what she did, the endless fascination of this particular strand of the medical profession, absorbed her and she found herself enjoying the round, explaining things for the students, answering questions directed at her by the boss.

When the round finished, Sally hurried off. Being on call at night didn't mean you could skip scheduled operations next morning, although this morning's roster was such that the third-year resident could do most of the work. And the first-year could assist while she had a small snooze standing up, a technique she'd perfected early in her career.

'Dr Cochrane?'

The department head, who appeared to be haunting her this week, once again materialised by her side in the corridor.

'I like my team to work in harmony,' he said bluntly. 'While I don't think it's necessary to socialise on a regular basis—in fact, as you know from my introductory statement, I believe teams work better if they don't fraternise all the time—perhaps if we all get together some time soon, we can thrash out a few things.'

He paused, and Sally looked up to see he was looking at her with a puzzled expression on his face.

'Thrash out a few things?' she repeated, equally puzzled.

He shook his head as if to clear it, then rubbed his temple as if he had a headache, but didn't elaborate.

'Organise it, will you? Miss Flintock has my diary. She'll tell you when I'm free,' he added, then he turned and walked, silently, away.

CHAPTER TWO

ONE year to go, Sally told herself. Less than that, in fact, to finish out her required time on the specialist programme, but there were still the final exams.

And she was on contract for the year.

Just one more year.

The words repeated themselves in her head as she hurried towards the theatres.

'Aha! Finally a body worth watching! I was just telling Fred here that this mixed-sex dressing room was a dead loss as far as us orthopods are concerned. Not a single woman on the programme at the moment.'

The men in the room, a mix of neuro and orthopedic residents and interns, all turned to see who'd entered.

Sally, whose three brothers had inured her to the sight of half-naked men, snorted at Warren Clarke's remark but didn't bite, remembering instead the clothing mix-up.

'You wouldn't know anything about the labels on the boxes being switched, I suppose?' she demanded.

He grinned at her.

'Catch you, did I?'

'Only once!' Sally told him. 'I'll check the tags in future. And if you think I looked stupid in a double large, imagine my lord and master in extra small.'

'Lord and master, Dr Cochrane?'

Uh-oh!

The soft question spun Sally around, to come face to face with the man himself.

Again.

'Y-you should wear a b-bell,' she stuttered, while the oth-

22

ers chuckled at her discomfort. 'On a collar around your neck like cats do to stop them bothering birds. What are you doing here, anyway?'

He looked down at her, and raised one dark, neatly formed eyebrow.

'Do I have to answer that question?'

Sally felt her muscles cringe, but she was in so deep, she might as well keep going.

'This morning's session is routine stuff,' she spluttered. 'Jerry can handle most of it. I thought you were listed for this afternoon—for Mrs Franklin's implant and Matt Crane's meningioma—as demonstration operations. We don't have students in Theatre this morning.'

'I *am* listed for this afternoon,' he agreed with perfect composure. 'But as yet I haven't had an opportunity to see Dr Finch perform, so, if it's all right with you, I shall join the surgical team.'

He lifted a set of clothes from the 'large' box, checked the tag, and proceeded to the back of the room where he always changed.

The cringe became a weakness, a liquefying of her bones, and Sally slumped onto the bench and breathed deeply. Perhaps one year *was* too long.

But the end of January was too late to be looking for a new position, so she was stuck with Grant Hudson.

No, not stuck with, but honoured to work in his team, she reminded herself firmly. Hadn't she welcomed the announcement of his arrival? To be able to say she'd trained under him, even if it was only for a year, would certainly enhance her job prospects when she was finally qualified.

What could she do in the meantime?

How was she going to get through the year?

'For a start, watch your mouth!' she muttered angrily under her breath, then she continued the lecture in her head.

That way, if he continues to materialise behind your back when you least expect it, you won't get caught out.

And, secondly, put any idea that it's attraction making you edgy right out of your head! Even if he didn't disapprove of team fraternisation, the last thing you need at the moment is a relationship with *any* man! Work, study, passing the exams. Those are your priorities this year! No diversions and no exceptions.

Grant changed swiftly, then, instead of heading for the scrub room, turned left along the clean corridor to where a wall phone was conveniently hung. He stabbed in the numbers of his own extension.

'Miss Flintock,' he said, hoping the phone would smooth the growl out of his voice, 'set up an appointment for me with whoever's in charge of Administration—Dickson, isn't it? A.s.a.p. Tell him I want to talk about the mixed dressing rooms. Page me when he's available.'

He dropped the phone back onto its cradle. He'd get rid of this combined changing room idea if it was the last thing he did.

Though why the sight of Sally Cochrane's slim brown legs should be affecting him so badly, he didn't know. The breasts he could understand. Pert, swelling breasts, their tan accentuated by the sensible white bra, were enough to stir any male's libido. In fact, he'd be worried if he wasn't affected just slightly by them.

But for the legs to be putting fantasies in his head?

Not to mention causing inappropriate reactions in his body!

When he knew how disastrous intra-team relationships could be?

Stress, that was what was causing it. Stress brought on by Tom's disappearance, Jocelyn's reaction, and exacerbated by the continuing headache and ankle pain he was suffering.

But the explanation didn't banish his mental image of Dr Cochrane's legs!

He groaned quietly to himself and pushed through the doors into the scrub room.

'Did you know males think about sex every eight seconds?' Jerry Finch's question, directed at the scrub nurse, was perfect synergy!

'Every eight seconds?' the nurse, whom Grant didn't recognise, echoed in horror. 'You'd have no time to think of anything else.'

She smiled a welcome to Grant and asked, 'Do you believe it, Doctor?'

'Definitely not,' he said stoutly, blocking from his mind the visual reminder of tanned skin pulled taut over swelling calves. He grinned at the nurse. 'I can go at least ten seconds.'

'Holding your breath? Standing on one leg?' a soft voice asked. Was Sally Cochrane getting her own back in the 'silent approach' department?

'Without thinking about sex,' Jerry said helpfully. 'It's a man thing.'

'Undoubtedly,' Sally retorted, but the glance she threw Grant's way was puzzled, as if she found it hard to believe he could indulge in a little light banter.

Serve her right for pre-judging him, he thought, although he couldn't alleviate a little stab of disappointment that she might have classified him as humourless.

Well, it beat thinking about sex!

Four hours later Sally was still puzzling over the man. He'd stayed to watch half an hour of Jerry's work then excused himself. No doubt to have a sleep before the afternoon session.

'You assisting him this afternoon?' Jerry asked her later.

They were in adjoining shower cubicles, yelling over the partition.

'No. He's got Andy lined up for it, and no doubt Daniel will make sure he's there.'

'Good luck to Andy, then,' Jerry said. 'I don't know about you, but I find the man unnerving. Can you imagine trying to do a stereotaxic procedure with him looking over your shoulder?'

Sally shuddered. Stereotaxic neuro-radiography was performed using an X-ray to guide a fine needle into a particular part of the brain. It required intense concentration and a steady hand.

'My hand shakes just thinking about it,' she admitted, then remembered she'd made a vow to keep her mouth shut. For all he should have gone home to sleep, the way Grant Hudson was haunting her, he was probably standing outside the door.

She turned off the shower, wrapped herself in a towel and opened it to check.

Safe!

She ducked back in to dry herself and pull on some clean underwear before venturing out to retrieve her clothes from her locker.

'He's very good,' she added to Jerry. 'I watched him clip an aneurysm last week. Talk about speedy fingers. And so neatly done I felt inadequate.'

'Janey was scrubbing for him. She said the same thing. Said she barely had the clip on the forceps and he was finished.'

Jane Dawson, Jerry's fiancée, was one of the hospital's top theatre nurses and Ted had fought hard to keep her for neuro work.

'He wants a gathering of all the neuro staff—well, the medical side of it,' Sally told Jerry, knowing he'd pick up on who 'he' was. 'Probably to tell us we all have to pull together. That Daniel will be lucky if I don't pull off his ears.'

'Don't bite when he teases you,' Jerry suggested. 'He only does it because he knows he'll get a rise.'

'He only does it because I'm a woman!' Sally retorted. 'I wish the new boss would consider splitting the team. Let Daniel take one strand and me the other.'

'Perhaps you should suggest it,' Jerry said. 'Once Chris Simpson gets back from the UK, it'd be worth thinking about.'

Chris Simpson was the second-year resident who made up their numbers in the small training unit, but because he was due back in a couple of months, no extra resident had been appointed.

'And you could ask for me and give Andy to Daniel.' Jerry was sounding quite excited by the idea. 'Dr Hudson would have to approve it.'

'And Daniel might not want Andy!' Sally added, gloom returning as she thought through the implications of any changes.

Andy Spence was a brilliant man and a skilled surgeon, but already, three years before he took his final neuro exams, he was looking ahead to a different future. Stereoscopic radiography wasn't new, but the use in brain surgery of the three-dimensional images it produced was still limited. Andy was bent on expanding it, and on delivering clearer and more detailed images for the surgeon.

'When's this get-together?' Jerry asked, and clear and detailed images of another surgeon suddenly filled Sally's head.

'I have to check with his secretary to find out when he's free. I'll let you know.'

She'd see the woman now, then grab something to eat, do a ward round and maybe, just maybe, get away early for a change.

Miss Flintock greeted her with a grimace and a nod of her head towards the inner sanctum.

So the bear was in his lair, was he? Sally's senses went on full alert.

'I've got to organise for him to see all the staff together,' she whispered to the older woman.

'So he said,' Miss Flintock said, sniffily enough to indicate displeasure.

Oh, dear!

'He probably doesn't realise you always did those things for Ted,' Sally said in her most soothing tones. '*I'm* quite happy for you to arrange it.'

'No. He said you're to do it, so you do it.' The words 'and don't expect any co-operation from me' remained unspoken but nonetheless implicit in the statement.

Sally closed her eyes and prayed for patience.

'So, when's he free?'

Miss Flintock shrugged her bony shoulders.

'How should I know? He tells me nothing. Nothing. First I'm supposed to screen his phone calls, only putting through people on the list. She was on the list. How was I supposed to know she was an impostor?'

Trying to follow the conversation was akin to walking in quicksand. Or perhaps it's because I'm tired, Sally decided.

'He must have a diary. Something that might show what he's doing when. Can't you check? He sounded as if he wanted this meeting soon.'

But Miss Flintock's folded arms told Sally she'd asked the wrong question. Was she supposed to pursue the grievance the secretary had aired? Provide a sympathetic ear? What had she said? Something about an impostor?

The sound of a phone being slammed back into its cradle and the faint echo of a colourful oath came clearly through the door and Sally, fearing her boss would emerge before she had the information she wanted, leaned forward and whispered, with what she hoped was sufficient menace, 'Just tell me when he's free, Miss Flintock. Now!'

Perhaps slamming down phone receivers was becoming a habit, Grant decided. That made twice in as many hours.

He rolled his chair back from his desk and massaged his scalp with his fingers. Hard.

And as if he didn't have enough problems, there was someone whispering in the outer office. No doubt Miss Flintock telling one of her cohorts just how badly she'd been treated.

Malice prompted by lack of sleep, fear for Tom and the frustration of the new job, brought him to his feet, and with the silent tread so deplored by his new senior resident he crossed to the door and flung it open.

Sally Cochrane was leaning across Miss Flintock's desk, her face fierce enough to suggest that her next move would be strangulation.

'Dr Cochrane?'

She shot upright so quickly her short, shiny brown hair seemed to bounce on her head.

'M-Miss F-Flintock's just checking your diary for me,' she stammered. 'To see when you're free. For the get-together.'

Grant struggled with the smile that wanted to spread across his face. A couple of times today he'd caught her out, but this was the first time he'd seen her disconcerted about it.

'And you were helping her look. Reading it upside down.' He glanced deliberately towards the desk, knowing full well the diary wasn't there. He'd taken it into his office when he'd phoned Administration to argue, unsuccessfully as it turned out, for an immediate meeting to discuss the changing rooms.

Sally gave him a wrathful glare, then flung up her arms.

'Arrange your bloody meeting yourself,' she said, then she stormed out the door, slamming it viciously behind her.

He stared at the still vibrating panel and allowed the smile to appear. He knew exactly how she felt.

'What language. I'm sorry you had to hear that, Doctor. Not that it's like Sally. She's usually the easiest of people to deal with. Although she does work too hard, and all those brothers of hers to worry about. Sex, drugs and rock and roll, you know.'

Miss Flintock's lips, pursed tight in disapproval, intrigued Grant even more than the strange phrase, but he had no intention of discussing the personal life of one of his staff with his secretary or anyone else.

'My diary is on my desk,' he said instead. 'Perhaps you could fix a time for me to get together with the other doctors on the team.' He hesitated, the 'sex, drugs and rock and roll' words still beating in his head. 'A breakfast meeting later in the week—that'd be the thing.'

He nodded to Miss Flintock and was about to leave the office when he realised he already had breakfast meetings with various of the other department heads lined up for later in the week.

'Better still, make it tomorrow.' He hesitated, not knowing his way around the hospital well enough to designate a room. 'The cafeteria at seven. We can eat and talk. Keep things informal.'

He walked away, the weariness in his legs reminding him of how little sleep he'd had. And the day had barely begun. He had surgery this afternoon, then tonight he was meeting Jocelyn for dinner. After standing her up last night, he'd better not forget.

But it wasn't Jocelyn's image in his head as he slumped down at his desk. It was that of a small sprite of a woman, with glossy dark hair—with a temper to match the fire in her eyes.

He smiled, then remembered all the reasons he didn't get involved with women on his team. No way!

Ever!

* * *

Sally forgot about lunch and opted for a round of patient visits instead. The sooner she got away from the hospital, the less chance she'd have of running into Grant Hudson—and copping a lecture on irrational behaviour!

She shouldn't have slammed the door, but the man made her so mad!

Calm down, Sally, breathe deeply.

She checked Craig Greenway in ICU first. His wound looked healthy, his body healing itself, but still no messages were getting through to his hands or feet.

'If you need the bed he can go down to a ward,' she told Ian Wheeler, the charge nurse on duty.

'Maybe tomorrow,' Ian agreed. 'Though we'd like to see some movement before we send him on. Matter of personal achievement.'

Sally grinned at him. 'I know exactly how you feel.'

The smile slipped a little as Grant walked in.

He nodded to Sally but spoke to Ian, which was just as well as her mouth had gone unaccountably dry.

Fear of retribution for the door-slamming? Or something else?

'No change?'

Ian shook his head.

'Well, we can't expect miracles,' Grant said easily. 'You still here, Dr Cochrane? I thought you'd have headed home to catch up on some sleep. You're not on duty tonight, are you?'

It was Sally's turn to shake her head. If she hadn't known better, she'd have assumed he was concerned about her.

'I'm on call for emergencies, but during the week that's almost a guarantee of a good night's sleep. Whoever's on duty can usually handle whatever comes in,' she told him.

A slight smile acknowledged her remark, then his eyes scanned her face before he spoke again.

'Miss Flintock will be contacting you about the meeting Breakfast tomorrow at seven in the cafeteria suit you?'

His voice was as bland as milk, but two could play that game.

Sally nodded, then decided she should leave before this nodding and head-shaking became a habit. Though it beat speech, given the dry-mouth thing.

She pulled herself together with an effort.

'See you later,' she said, uttering the meaningless phrase to the air between the two men.

But as she walked towards the lift, a tension between her shoulder blades, and a prickle of electricity along her nerves, warned her escape wasn't going to be so easy.

He'd caught up with her again.

'We're a small specialty compared with most, so we have to work closely together.' He spoke as he came alongside, launching into the subject as if continuing an interrupted conversation. 'That's one of the reasons I don't promote a lot of socialising between my staff. We need to see other people to avoid becoming too focussed on what we do, to the exclusion of everything else.'

'You made that clear in your initial memorandum,' Sally reminded him, though she was wondering, if that was one of the reasons, what the others were. 'No fraternisation.'

He frowned as if underlings talking back to him was unexpected.

'I'm sure I didn't put it that bluntly,' he told her. 'But I've experienced what can happen when a personal relationship between two members of a team goes wrong—disastrously wrong—and how disruptive it can be for everyone on the team.'

Sally would have liked to point out that adults should be able to separate the work and play sections of their lives, but as he was frowning down at her she remembered her own mental warning and kept quiet.

'That doesn't mean I don't want the team to work to-gether,' the man continued. 'Friction between members can interfere with concentration, and I'm sure I don't need to remind you, Dr Cochrane, how important concentration is in an operating theatre. Particularly in our field.'

They'd reached the lifts and Sally turned towards him, hoping her face didn't reveal the satisfaction she was feeling. Talk about heaven-sent opportunities.

'If you're worried that Daniel's niggling will upset my concentration, why not split the team?'

Blue eyes, bright with intelligence, gleamed for an instant, but his face remained composed. No flicker of a grin—of any emotion!

'I am not worried about Daniel's niggling, as you call it, upsetting your concentration, because I expect you to control your reactions to him. He's your direct superior, Dr Cochrane. It's his duty to instruct and inform you. Reacting with smart remarks or threats of violence is hardly mature behaviour, would you say?'

Hope withered in Sally's chest, replaced by an urge to show this man exactly how violent she could be.

'I assume he will also receive a little pep talk from you,' she said, wondering why she'd ever found such cold blue eyes attractive. 'Perhaps about showing proper respect to—'

About to say 'female members of the team' she stopped abruptly. That was to close to telling the tales Daniel had already accused her of carrying.

'Me,' she finished lamely.

The lift arrived and the doors opened.

'Have you considered it might be the way you treat him? I find him perfectly respectful,' Grant Hudson remarked, ushering Sally into the lift ahead of him.

'That's not respect, that's toadying,' she muttered in reply.

'Interested in animals, Dr Cochrane?' the aggravating man said. 'I remember hearing someone else likened to a bear.'

The lift had stopped again, and Sally, heedless of the floor, stepped out and walked away, hoping she looked as if she had a reason for striding towards the… She looked around. Delivery suites! Great.

Her heart was pounding, and the air she breathed felt heavy in her lungs.

Please, let it be from lack of sleep, not Grant Hudson. Or from his reprimand, not his physical presence.

He was no more interested in her than he was in any other member of the team, and a bout of unrequited love would be more disastrous to her work and study plans than pneumonia! Surely fate couldn't be so unkind?

Not now!

She turned into a washroom, fortunately empty, and leaned her forehead on the cool glass of a mirror.

For ten years, since a wildly romantic rush of adolescent love had so distracted her from her studies she'd nearly missed the scholarship she'd been seeking, she'd put her career ahead of her social life. Ahead of everything, until her mother's illness had intervened. Now she had a year to make up—one year before she reached the goal she'd worked towards for so long.

Once she'd begun studying, physical urges had been dampened down by her determination to be the best she could.

The physical side of things with Greg hadn't been that great anyway. In fact, love-making had proved a disappointment, and she'd been happy to forego it.

So why should her aging—if at thirty it could be described as aging—body suddenly start reacting to a man?

To that man in particular?

Not that she fancied him. In fact, he was so aggravating, she was more likely to clock him one than kiss him.

She shuddered as one single word again pricked her slumbering flesh into a little shimmy of excitement.

The mirror failed to provide answers so she washed her hands and splashed water on her face, then left the sanctuary of the washroom and headed for the ward. One quick check on the ward patients then she was off.

CHAPTER THREE

'IF WE all got the message, how come the boss didn't?'

Seven in the morning and the team was assembled, an assortment of breakfasts, indicative of personal choice, in front of them.

Daniel asked the obvious and Sally shrugged.

'He certainly knew because he told me about it.'

'He's not in Theatre now,' Andy said. 'But he was still at the hospital last night when the first of the freeway accident victims came in, so heaven knows what time he got home.'

'I was there as well, in case you don't remember standing beside me,' Sally reminded him. 'I'm sure there used to be nights on call when nothing happened, but this week…'

'He was up in the ICU early this morning,' one of the young interns offered. 'I saw him checking on the fellow in the revolving bed.'

'I could phone ICU and ask if he's there,' Jerry suggested, but Sally shook her head.

'If he's there, he must be busy, so we shouldn't interrupt him.'

'I'll go up and see.' Daniel left them at the table, and Sally felt an easing of her tension.

'I think the boss wanted to talk about us working as a team,' she said. 'Little pep talk about pulling together, treating each other with courtesy and getting on with things without getting too tied up with each other.'

'He's back on the fraternisation among the staff, is he?' Jerry rolled his eyes in mock disbelief. 'That'd be OK if we ever had time to see anyone outside the hospital—and outside the theatre and the neuro ward. When we're not working, we're studying, or writing papers, or trying to catch up on reading. I've a pile of recent journals on my floor you couldn't jump over.'

'You've still had time to get engaged,' Andy reminded him.

'Pure convenience,' Jerry retorted. 'Once you're engaged you don't have to go out nearly as much. You've got the excuse of saving up for the wedding, and then the house.'

Sally finished her breakfast, only half listening to the conversation eddying around the table. Until something Paul was saying caught her attention.

Something about why Grant Hudson frowned on fraternising within the team.

'And my brother worked with him for a while in Sydney. Apparently, back when Dr Hudson was a resident he had this torrid relationship with a woman who was the neuro registrar. Went on for years, then she threw him over for the department head.'

'That sounds like gossip, and if there's one thing this hospital doesn't need, it's more gossip,' Sally told him.

Paul did an affronted look.

'It's true. I can't remember her name but she married a guy called Binstead.'

'Isn't there a Lance Binstead on the council of the College of Surgeons?' Jerry asked.

'That's him!' Paul said, his tone revealing how pleased he was to have back-up for the story.

But Sally's mind had drifted down another path, and she felt an uneasiness in her chest as she considered the blow such a defection would have been to a man as proud as Grant Hudson. It certainly made the no-fraternisation rule easier to understand.

Though imagining him in love with anyone was difficult. Upsetting. But Grant Hudson thrown over in love? Impossible!

The mere thought of it filled her with an inexplicable sadness.

But why should she care?

She sighed, then put his problems out of her mind to concentrate on her own.

She'd been relieved when he hadn't shown up. In Theatre last night, she'd been able to ignore the physical manifestations his presence was causing her. Concentration formed its own barrier. But in daylight? At a casual breakfast meeting?

The less she saw of him the better, she told herself, but deep inside, almost in the region of her heart, was a gnawing sense of concern.

A barely heard whisper that said, Let him be all right. Let it not be an accident that's kept him.

'That you buzzing, Sally?'

Jerry's question brought her back to reality. She pulled her pager out of her pocket and studied the message.

'I've to call his office. Hold on and I'll let you know what's happening.'

She crossed to a phone and dialled the extension.

'Sally, it's Jill Flintock. I came in early to get some filing done because with the new man in the job and trying to tell him how things work, I don't get time during the day...'

Sally closed her eyes and waited, assuming Miss Flintock would eventually get to the point.

'And as I was here I answered the phone. Then I tried to contact him. Dr Hudson. Could you ask him to check his pager? He must have it switched off or it's low on batteries or something. I've been trying to page him and then I tried to get him on his mobile number but nothing's working.'

Miss Flintock sounded rattled—a rare occurrence.

Sally hesitated, uncertain whether to further alarm the woman, then decided she had to know.

'I can't ask him to check anything. He hasn't shown up,' she said. 'Have you tried his home number?'

'I did that before I called you.'

An image of Grant Hudson's body lying on his bathroom floor, blood oozing from a head wound, flashed through Sally's mind. She'd never seen his bathroom, but in the image the tiles were blue. The blood a vivid scarlet.

'There could be a simple explanation,' she told Miss Flintock. 'Why were you looking for him?'

'He wanted to speak to Mr Dickson about the changing rooms and had an appointment at eight, but Mr Dickson's secretary's just phoned and says he won't be able to make it.'

'Mr Dickson's not the right person anyway,' Sally said, wondering why Grant Hudson should be concerned about the changing rooms. 'It's the surgical division of the medical advisory committee who organises theatre usage. He should have talked to Flo, the theatre secretary.'

'Oh, I don't think he'd like that,' Miss Flintock said. 'He's a man who likes to go straight to the top.'

Sally gave a grim chuckle.

'If he wants any favours in Theatres he'd better learn, and learn quickly, that Flo *is* the top, no matter how many letters other people might have in their titles or after their names.'

Miss Flintock actually laughed, which was tantamount to agreeing—although she wouldn't have been disloyal enough to put agreement into words.

'So what will I do about him?'

'Don't panic. If his eight-o'clock appointment has cancelled he can afford to be a little late.'

'But he's never late,' she heard Miss Flintock say, more to herself than to Sally, then the click told her they'd been disconnected.

She returned to the remnants of her now cold breakfast and picked at it, knowing in this job you ate when time was available. Though today that theory had little appeal. The non-appearance of the new boss was causing too much internal unease.

'So? What's the explanation? Why has the great man stood us up?' Andy asked.

Sally hesitated.

'We don't know.' She looked around at the 'team'. With the registrar, and first- and third-year residents, plus the two interns in the hospital, Neuro was well covered.

'Actually, you might ask Daniel to start the ward round if the boss doesn't turn up, and I'll go and see Miss Flintock. She's panicking because she's lost him. But, whatever you do, don't start a fuss about his absence. You can imagine how he'd react if he arrives to find a full alert out for him.'

With the recurring image of his body on the blue tiles of a bathroom she hadn't seen, she knew she'd have to check his home.

If Miss Flintock would part with his address.

'Oh, Sally, I'd be so pleased if you'd go over there,' the secretary said in answer to her suggestion. 'What if he's ill? He's had a headache for a few days now, and he's been limping from time to time as if he's in pain. Or he could have slipped in the bathroom and hit his head. I've got this dreadful mental picture of him lying unconscious on the floor.'

'On what colour tiles?' Sally asked, although she knew it was immaterial and there was no way Grant Hudson could be beaming a picture of himself in distress to both of them.

Miss Flintock looked startled, then puzzled.

'On the floor where he's lying,' Sally expanded.

'It's black and white, my picture,' Miss Flintock said, then she reverted to her usual Miss Efficiency role and passed Sally a scrap of paper with an address on it. 'He lives in a block of apartments overlooking the river. You'll probably have to see the manager to get in.'

Sally took the note and checked the address. Only a few

streets from where she lived herself, though definitely on the better side of the tracks. A journey of ten minutes max as she'd be going against the traffic.

'I'll let you know,' she promised Miss Flintock, 'but, in the meantime, it might be best if you can keep his absence quiet. He probably has a perfectly logical explanation for being late and will be furious with both of us if he finds we've started a panic.'

'You're right, of course,' Miss Flintock said, so gloomily Sally wondered just how often Grant had stepped on the older woman's toes.

If he'd been more approachable she could have talked to him about how to handle his secretary...

Or if she hadn't been wary of spending too much time in his presence, given her strange reactions to the man!

Enough! Going out to check he wasn't lying injured on his bathroom floor was one thing. Telling him how to sweet-talk his secretary was a whole different ball game.

She pulled into the visitors' parking area of the tall high-rise apartment block and looked out over the single row of houses below it to the wide stretch of river. From higher up the view must be breathtaking.

Not that she had time to think about views.

Uneasiness, accelerated by Grant Hudson's reaction if he did happen to be at home and *not* unconscious, dogged her footsteps as she dashed towards the front entrance.

'Try the rational way first,' she told herself, and searched the bank of buttons at the side of the front entrance. Unit 33. She rang the bell, then nearly fell over when Grant's voice answered.

'I'll buzz you in. Come on up. Tenth floor.'

She glanced up and saw the security camera and knew he must have seen her face as he'd answered. So why not ask what she wanted? Why just let her in?

Speaking of getting in, she'd better go now, before the

front door release clicked back into place and locked her out again.

Bemused and bewildered, she entered a spacious, plant-lined foyer, crossed the marble tiles and summoned the lift.

It was on the foyer level, and the doors slid open. She pressed '10', and stood, eyeing her reflection in the shiny metal panels, wondering if she'd stepped into another dimension, so weird was this situation.

Unit 33 was on the right as she stepped out, and she guessed it would face east towards the river. The door opened as she approached, and Grant Hudson, clad only in a towel if you didn't count the plaster on his left ankle, stood before her.

He was propped on crutches but what drew her eyes were the stitches on his chin.

Concern overrode all other emotions.

'Oh, you *were* hurt. Miss Flintock and I were worried. We thought you might have been. Was it a car accident?'

She stepped forward, automatically reaching out a hand to touch the scar, then stopped abruptly and frowned at the man.

'You're not Grant, not Dr Hudson.'

The stranger smiled.

'Well, if you want a Dr Hudson, I am one. I take it from your surprise you're not the new cleaning lady.'

Sally shook her head.

Definitely another dimension.

Although the main cause for concern still remained.

'Where is he? Where's Grant—Dr Hudson? He had a seven o'clock appointment, and an eight o'clock, and didn't turn up for either, even though the eight o'clock was cancelled. No one answered when Miss Flintock phoned here.'

The second Dr Hudson smiled and Sally remembered just how attractive her Dr Hudson had looked on the rare occasion she'd seen him do likewise.

Though this one didn't send feathery tickles down her spine, which, given the likeness, was particularly peculiar.

'He was out rescuing his lost brother from the talons of a conniving female,' the man said, although the softness of his voice suggested he hadn't found the female conniving, and possibly hadn't been in need of rescue.

'I've been lost, you see,' he added, which didn't help Sally at all. 'Sam found me, then she found Grant and it was like one of those card games you play where you match up pairs. She matched us up and Grant whisked me away to this place. Then he dashed off to work, leaving instructions for me to let in the cleaning lady—to save the manager doing it.'

He glanced down at his attire and said, 'Mind you, I shouldn't have greeted the cleaning lady looking like this. Perhaps I should change.'

He's obviously quite deranged, Sally decided. And if he really had been missing, it was no wonder Grant Hudson had been worried. Which might go some way to explaining his tetchiness.

She grabbed the stranger's arm as he backed away, not wanting to wait while he found some clothes to put on.

'Where's Grant now?' Sally asked, speaking slowly and clearly so this copy of her boss would understand.

'He's just left for the hospital,' the copy said. 'You probably passed him on the way if that's where you've come from. Are you his secretary? No, of course you're not. You're wearing a white coat.'

His blue eyes, so like his brother's but lacking the power to affect her breathing, gleamed with conjecture.

'Something going on between you and him that you've come rushing over to see if he's OK?'

'No, there's nothing going on!' Sally said crossly. 'Not now, and not ever.'

'Well, that's a pity,' the man said. 'The old fellow needs a woman in his life. I can understand why he took the busi-

ness with Erica hard. Wretched woman took him for a ride
Then he had that disastrous problem on his team. But to
swear off women for life…'

He studied her again for a moment, then frowned.

'Although he hasn't been here for long, has he? Hardly
time to win a pretty woman like you. Am I right about that
or have I lost more time than I realised? He hasn't been here
long?'

'This is his second week,' Sally said, anxious to help the
confused being.

'That's what I thought,' he said, with surprising relief. '
had a fall,' he continued. 'Ended up with amnesia. Not a lot
of fun—it leaves such gaps. That's why it was great to not
only see Grant this morning but to recognise who he was—
to really know him.'

Sally put her hand to her head and massaged her throbbing
temples.

'I—I'd better go,' she stammered. 'Get back to work. Nice
to meet you. Goodbye.'

And on that note she fled, hurrying back to the lift, press
ing the button, thankful no one had needed it since she'd
arrived so the doors immediately opened and she all but tum
bled inside.

'So he's got a twin,' she said to herself as she was carried
downwards. 'That's not so rare.'

But the experience of meeting the man who was, yet
wasn't, Grant Hudson had shaken her.

Her! Unshakeable Sally Cochrane! Wouldn't her brothers
laugh if they knew?

Not that they ever would.

Grant made it to the hospital a little after nine. To avoid Miss
Flintock's recriminations about the two meetings he'd
missed—and had only remembered he'd missed as he'd
driven into the car park—he went straight to the ward. He'd

deal with Miss Flintock later. For now, it was enough that Tom was safe.

Or was it? He sighed as the lift took him up to the ward. The relief he should have felt from finding Tom was counterbalanced by his concern over any long-lasting neurological damage his twin might have suffered. And the illness was another worry.

Though from the way he'd been looking at the woman who'd found him, maybe he'd found the one person who'd cure his wanderlust.

In the tearoom, the pre-round meeting was under way. He nodded to the assembly, sat down in the one vacant chair and waved his hand to indicate to Jerry to continue talking.

He looked around, figured that Daniel had taken his place and Jerry was doing the explanations Sally Cochrane usually handled.

He waited for a break to ask the obvious.

''Where's Dr Cochrane? She's on duty today, isn't she?'

'Hmm, not like Sally to be late,' Jerry Finch remarked, but, although he looked down at his watch as he spoke, Grant caught the glance he sent the assembled staff.

There was something going on here—and, whatever it was, they suspected he wouldn't like it.

'So, who's next up?' he asked Jerry.

'Mrs Franklin had a good night, although she's feeling tenderness on the site of the implant. She woke early and a nurse has been working with her on the control box, keeping note of the settings as she trials them. No new problems arising from the operation.'

He looked up and Grant nodded for him to continue. These meetings were to brief him on changes in patient status prior to the round. No problems meant there were no warning signs or signals they had to consider.

'Craig Greenway was transferred to the ward last night. His wound still looks healthy, vital signs good, still no response to stimuli, although he claims he can tense his shoulder muscles and actually feel them moving.'

'So far no one's observed this phenomenon,' Daniel put in, and Grant, hearing a shadow of disdain in the words, understood why the registrar would irritate a straight-shooter like Sally Cochrane.

And where was she?

After all, he'd called a staff meeting for seven. She should have been in early, not late.

Jerry's voice, continuing down the list of ward patients, should have reminded him to put aside the growing annoyance he was feeling, but he couldn't shake it. He hadn't explained why he'd missed the meeting, and no one had asked. Had none of them turned up?

And now he thought about it, Miss Flintock hadn't queried his absence when he'd phoned her as he'd waited for the lift to tell her he'd been unexpectedly delayed, but was now at work.

'Sorry I'm late.'

Sally Cochrane breezed in, sent a general smile in the direction of the assembly, then perched on the arm of Andy's chair.

'You can slope off if you want to,' she said to the resident, then she deigned to glance at Grant.

'If that's OK with Dr Hudson. Andy was on duty last night and caught most of the mayhem down in A and E. This morning he's been holding the fort for me,' she added, looking directly at Grant this time.

Then her brow puckered and she said, 'I know this will sound like a weird question, but what colour are your bathroom tiles?'

Weird didn't begin to describe her question. It was sufficiently bizarre to startle him out of his consideration of why his irritation with her hadn't been enough to dampen the sudden physical surge of awareness he was beginning to feel in her presence.

Had the woman taken leave of her senses?

Had he?

'White, I imagine. Aren't all bathrooms white?' He found himself frowning now. Why the hell had he answered her? 'Now, if you've finished organising my staff and checking on the interior decorating of my apartment, perhaps we could get to work.'

The words came out more crisply than he'd intended, for part of his mind had once again been distracted by the golden gleams in dark brown eyes and the heat they caused in his gut.

'Mr Andrews has also come down from the ICU. His latest scan suggests we got all the abscess and there's no continuing infection on the site,' Jerry continued.

'The bathroom in my little flat near the hospital has got green tiles, Sal, if you want to know,' Daniel murmured. 'Come up and see it some time.'

Grant saw Sally straighten with irritation. Time to forget golden gleams and take control here.

'As you know, Mr Andrews had a subdural abscess removed,' he said, directing his words at the interns. 'He presented with fever, headaches, some confusion. We aspirated it through a burr hole, and flushed the area with heavy doses of antibiotic. The fact that he's been transferred from the ICU indicates he's stable. What's the likely outcome for him?'

'Mental impairment?'

'Possibly, though in his case, considering the site, I doubt it. But what's more likely to cause him ongoing problems?'

'Epilepsy?' Paul Adams, another of the interns, supplied the answer, and Jerry expanded on this likelihood and the difficulty of balancing anti-epileptic drugs to suit each individual.

'We have to consider the patient's quality of life,' Sally

Cochrane told the two younger men. 'Why save that life if it means they have to live zonked out on drugs for the remainder of it?'

'I trust you're not advocating we don't save it, Dr Cochrane?'

Sally looked directly at him.

'No, but I believe we should take responsibility for prescribing the correct drug dosage, rather than leaving it to the patient's GP to struggle through the maze of combinations available,' she said, adding, after an infinitesimal pause, 'Sir.'

Grant guessed where she was coming from and privately agreed with her, but this wasn't the time or place for further discussion on the parameters of their responsibility.

'The GPs see the patient more regularly than we do so are more likely to know when an imbalance occurs,' he reminded her, 'but you're right. It is our responsibility to at least send home a stable patient.'

He glanced at his watch. 'We'd better move on. Any specific problems you feel should be brought to the team's attention?'

Daniel flipped through the cards.

'Miss Wingate, trigeminal nerve surgery for the relief of neuralgia last Friday, is complaining of a lack of feeling in her fingers.'

'In her fingers?' Grant shook his head.

'Yesterday it was her toes, and the day before that her knees and elbows were numb,' Sally told him. 'She lives alone and doesn't want to go home. Although she was managing quite well prior to the operation, first the pain of the neuralgia, and since then the disorientation following the operation, have undermined her confidence. She's on a waiting list for three different nursing homes, but with no family to put pressure on these places for her it's unlikely anything will come up in the immediate future.'

One of the problems of operating on elderly patients was

the effect of the anaesthetic on them. Grant wondered how they could help this woman who was obviously suffering from disorientation.

'How do things work here in Queensland? Can *we* put pressure on the nursing homes?'

'Sally's already doing that,' Jerry answered. 'But in the meantime, we can't realistically keep her in the neuro ward.'

'Why? Do we need the bed?'

'We've a set number of bed days allocated for each procedure,' Daniel reminded him. 'Commonwealth regulatory restrictions which apply to all hospitals.'

Grant was wondering how to address this when Sally spoke up.

'Tell him something he doesn't know,' she said crossly to Daniel. Then she turned to Grant. 'Waiting lists for elective surgery, which most neuralgia operations are considered to be, are fairly lengthy, but it's a lack of staff and available theatre hours rather than beds that cause the backlog. At the moment, in the ward, beds aren't a problem.'

Grant could feel the intensity in her words, and see it in the eyes focussed so directly on his face. It was almost as if she was challenging him. Daring him to make the final decision.

Well, he'd never been one for following *all* the rules.

'If we've a bed available, maybe we should check out the lack of feeling,' Grant suggested. 'Can you come up with some non-invasive and preferably inexpensive tests to cover our hides should anyone question her presence for a few more days?'

Sally nodded, surprise at this evidence of the man's humanity rendering her momentarily speechless.

'And ask the social work department to rustle up a longer list of suitable nursing homes. She should have her name down with more than three, but check she approves before they list her anywhere else. You might also remind the social work department it's their job to see to patients' long-term welfare. Get them doing the ring-around for you.'

Sally was about to remind *him* that the social work department had responsibility for the entire patient population of the hospital while they only had their handful of neuro patients to consider, but he was already on his feet, signalling that the time for talk was over.

Action man!

With a white-tiled bathroom!

He must have thought she'd taken leave of her senses, asking a question like that.

As he led the group out to the ward, Sally slipped behind to thank Andy for covering for her.

'No covering needed. He neither explained why he was late nor did he ask where you were—at least, not until well into the session.'

'Are you joining us, Dr Cochrane?'

Sally said a brief goodbye to her colleague then rejoined the team, her normal irritation with the new boss now back in place, no matter how understanding he'd seemed about Miss Wingate.

The round passed without incident, and Sally, who was due to assist in an orthopedic operation with possible nerve involvement, was heading for Theatre when Grant caught up with her.

Again.

'I'm sorry I didn't make the meeting this morning. Something…' The pause lengthened before he added, 'Personal came up.'

If she didn't tell him about her little expedition, his brother surely would.

'Like a lost brother?'

He looked so startled Sally chuckled.

'Miss Flintock was worried about you. I drove out to check. Met the carbon copy.'

She saw the alarm in his eyes and added, 'We didn't make a fuss. No one but Miss Flintock and the team knew you'd gone missing. Your eight-o'clock appointment was cancelled anyway.'

He said nothing, but the intent look he was giving her was unsettling, so she rattled on.

'Though it's no use talking to Dickson about anything pertaining to the theatres anyway. Flo, the theatre secretary, is the power in that department.'

The man threw up his arms in a gesture of pure frustration.

'The introductory booklet issued to staff should come with a special translation giving the real details of who's who,' he muttered. 'Nothing's what it seems in this place. And how did you know what I wanted to discuss with Mr Dickson?'

Sally stiffened. Best if she could ignore the final question, as she didn't want to get Miss Flintock into trouble with her boss. Concentrate on the first issue.

'This place, as you call it, is one of the best run and most successful hospitals in the state. Mainly,' she added, feeling compelled to defend her place of training, 'because the upper levels of staff have the good sense to delegate responsibility to those who have the most experience in each area. What does Ken Dickson know about theatre usage? Book-learning he might have, but in practice our theatre rosters and staffing arrangements work because Flo makes them work.'

'She won't make the mixed changing rooms work!' Grant Hudson fumed. 'Not if I have anything to say about it.'

Uh-oh!

'I'd better get going,' Sally said. 'I'm needed up in Theatre.'

And on that note she fled, although there'd be no permanent escape. Once he found out from Flo that it had been she who'd lobbied and nagged and plotted to get the trial of mixed dressing rooms, he'd... She didn't know how he'd react, although she suspected the skirmishes they'd had to date would escalate to open warfare.

Well, if that's what he wanted, that's what he'd get. Just because she was suddenly and unexpectedly beset by biological impulses and physiological reactions to the man, it didn't mean she couldn't hold her own in a battle.

Grant watched her scurry away. Conversations with Sally Cochrane, while usually illuminating in some way, rarely answered the questions he wanted answered. She had a knack of dragging in a bit of trivia to divert him along a different path.

Not that she'd succeeded this time. Flo, the theatre secretary, was the person he needed to see. And fighting for male rights in changing rooms should take his mind off his senior resident's legs. And gold-flecked eyes. And inappropriate physical reactions to same!

'Oh, I can't do anything to change the rooms now!' Flo said to him, after he'd spent two hours waiting—and plotting his attack—until she had time to fit him in to her schedule. 'It's a trial, you see. And trials have to run their course or they wouldn't be trials, now, would they? If, at the end of three months—that's how long we said the trial would be—you still feel uncomfortable changing in with women—not that your changing room would have many, only Sally and occasionally Brenda Watts, and maybe Sue Robertson—'

Flo beamed benevolently at him, and continued to flood the air with words.

'You can vote against it. Democratic, that's how we are here. It was the MSC—that's our Medical Specialists' Committee which comes under the MAC, the main Medical Advisory Committee—which decided to trial it. I'm minutes secretary of the MSC as well as theatre secretary, you know. It's the first time they've had the same person doing the two jobs but the MSC only meets once a month so it doesn't interfere with my job here.'

She paused for breath and Grant thanked her and hurried out of her office. Had she talked so much the first time he'd met her? On his introductory tour of the hospital?

And if she was always so garrulous, when did she find time to get her work done? Which she must do for, he had to admit, the theatres ran well.

He was in the corridor outside the secretary's office when the resident he was hoping to banish from his mind came bowling out of the clean area behind the theatres.

'Ha! Just the person I want to see,' he said, dismissing the avoidance tactics he'd been planning in favour of information-gathering. 'Are you going somewhere urgent or can you have lunch with me? I need someone to explain the workings of this hospital and, as you're its greatest advocate, who better?'

She looked so stunned he wondered if perhaps he'd taken the keeping-things-professional approach too far.

'It's only lunch,' he added softly. 'I'm lecturing at two so I won't keep you long.'

She glanced at her watch and he guessed she was calculating how many minutes, or possibly seconds, she'd be trapped in his company. The thought made him feel unaccountably upset. Time was when women had enjoyed having lunch with him.

'I suppose so,' she muttered, and the upset turned to pique.

'Well, don't force yourself!' he growled, and was surprised when she reacted with a chuckle.

'I'm sorry! I did make it sound as if a scale and clean at the dentist would be a better option. I've got to eat, so why not do it together? I wanted to ask you something anyway.'

She led the way towards the lift to take them down to the cafeteria.

'Are you at all interested in Parkinson's? To the extent of knowing much about the latest research? I know your field is pain, but I was reading somewhere about new surgical techniques for Parkinson's and knowing you were in the States last year—' Perhaps alerted by his silence, she broke off, looking up at him, the little gleams in her eyes dancing as she smiled.

'Talk too much, don't I?' she said. 'This was your call, your invitation. What did you want to know?'

She looked so contrite he found himself smiling.

'I'll look out some info on Parkinson's I did happen to pick up in the States last year, and there's an excellent website that's kept updated. I'll give you the location.'

If he'd expected gratitude he was doomed to disappointment, for Sally had greeted this kindly offer with a frown.

A distracted frown.

'He's not really very like you at all, is he?' she said, then she seemed to snap out of whatever world she'd entered, while a pink tide of confusion washed into her cheeks. 'Your brother…I was thinking… Yes, I'd like the website address,' she finished.

The lift deposited them on the ground floor and they joined the exiting throng. Sally hurried towards the cafeteria but Grant followed more slowly.

Why on earth would she have been thinking of Tom? She'd met him briefly, and had probably only admitted as much because she guessed Tom would tell him she'd called.

Yet there she'd stood, all pink-cheeked confusion, while he'd been at his most accommodating best, answering her question, sharing information with a colleague—developing, he thought, a better relationship between them.

Professionally, of course.

CHAPTER FOUR

STANDING next to Sally in the food queue, Grant again caught that hint of flowers. Not exactly a perfume. More a suggestion of the scented air one caught walking past a florist's shop. A tantalising pleasantness.

'Aren't you going to eat something?' she asked, jolting him out of his search for a simile to describe it exactly.

He glanced down at his tray and realised he'd been pushing it absent-mindedly along the rack, but hadn't managed to put anything on it.

'I'll have one of these,' he said, hiding his fluster by grabbing the closest offering in the refrigerated cabinet.

'Very healthy!' his companion said, her lips twitching as she observed the violent pink icing on the bun he'd selected.

'I was thinking of something else,' he told her, hoping she'd assume his thoughts were on work, not her perfume or the way his nerves felt more alert when in her presence.

He swapped the bun for a plate of sandwiches then held it out for her inspection.

'This better?'

She eyed them doubtfully.

'I guess so. I mean, the green stuff in the filling is undoubtedly lettuce but the pink goo in the middle one looks very like the icing on the bun. Is it something new they're trialling, do you think? The all-purpose, nutritionally balanced spread which goes with everything?'

By now, a male nurse behind Grant in the queue had become interested.

'Everything tastes the same anyway,' he offered, 'so why bother trying to disguise it with different colours?'

Totally put off by these comments, Grant shoved the sandwiches back into the cabinet.

'I'll settle for a cup of coffee,' he said firmly, then he glanced at Sally's tray. A bowl of salad, two small bread rolls, a tub of yoghurt, some sliced fruit and two apples were spread across it.

'The healthy food is right at the beginning,' she told him. 'But don't worry, we can share. If I get hungry later I always keep a packet of fruit bars in my locker. For those days when a lunch-hour seems like a distant memory and a lunch-minute is grabbed at three in the afternoon.'

'I don't think I'll ever forget those days,' Grant remarked, ordering his coffee then following his companion to the till. 'I remember the relief I felt when I made senior resident and finally registrar. Fewer nights on call, fewer trips down to A and E. Other people to do the running around that killed any hope of keeping to a schedule and having what might pass for a ''normal'' day.'

She looked up at him and smiled, the shift in expression lighting up her face, changing it from pretty to vividly attractive.

You don't get involved with women on your staff, he reminded himself, paying his bill, collecting his coffee then following the woman he wasn't going to get involved with to a table at the far side of the room.

Ever again!

She sat down and unloaded her tray, shifting one bread roll from the small plate to the edge of her coffee saucer. Then she piled half the salad onto the plate with the remaining bread roll and passed it to him.

'You didn't pick up any cutlery so you'll have to manage with the spoon,' she told him, waving away his protest that he couldn't share her lunch.

'Of course you can,' she told him. 'Eat.'

She toyed with her salad, finally choosing a tiny tomato

and raising it on her fork before glancing towards him and launching into a conversation that told him how firmly focussed her mind must be on work. No matter where his had strayed!

'There's something else I wanted to ask about, and it kind of follows on from what you were saying about the workload. I've been wondering how much busier this unit has to get before the powers that be—' a half-grin told him she included him in that description '—might consider splitting Neuro into two teams. If we had another first-year and Andy under Daniel, and the second-year, when Chris comes back, and Jerry working with me, it might make the scheduling easier and also cut the workload on individuals.'

She popped the tomato into her mouth and Grant, his attention distracted by the small red globe disappearing between even white teeth, failed to respond.

'Of course, we'd have to negotiate more theatre time,' she continued, when the tomato had been dealt with, 'but, in my opinion, treating pain-relief surgery as elective is totally unacceptable. Those patients shouldn't be regarded as urgently as an aneurysm or brain tumour, but certainly not shuffled to the end of the line, their operations put off again and again because an emergency takes their allotted theatre time.'

Her passion was like a call to battle and he smiled.

'It's like an echo of words I used to my department head when I was a resident about a hundred years ago,' he told her.

'Poor old man!' she murmured, the golden glints in her eyes teasing his senses. 'You must be what? All of thirty-five? Six?'

'Close to that,' he admitted. She was thirty. He knew that from her personnel file. If he told her thirty-six would she think a six-year age difference too much?

Too much for what? his common sense yelled in his head. You don't get involved with staff, remember? Especially not staff who have very important exams looming later in the year.

And she hasn't shown the slightest interest in you anyway! More interest in Tom, if you look at it clearly!

He hauled his mind back to business.

'Not that my failure to change the status of pain patients at my previous hospital should put us off starting a similar campaign here,' he said, and silently congratulated himself on his control. 'Though we'll have to work undercover, so to speak. I've had enough experience of hospital politics to know a new boy can't go barging in and demanding long lists of reforms.'

He tried another smile and hoped it was more professional than the previous one had been.

'In fact, it's what I wanted to discuss. Let's start with the inimitable Flo.'

He was watching Sally as he spoke—in fact, if the truth be known, he was watching Sally far more often than he should. But, be that as it may, watching her meant he caught a slight tightening of her lips, and a sudden wariness in the wide brown eyes.

'She's very good at what she does,' his colleague told him. 'Excellent, in fact. When Ted was here—Dr Watson, your predecessor—she's the one who kept him on time, and paged him when he was due in Theatre and generally kept his mind on the job, although his passion for fishing and his plans for his post-retirement around-Australia fishing trip were demanding more and more of his attention.'

Around-Australia fishing trips? Grant gazed at his informant. Was it the mention of Flo, whose words did just that, which had started a similar flood of useless information from his senior resident?

'You've already convinced me Flo is the power in that area,' he said, hoping to sound businesslike enough to get Sally back on track. 'What I'd like to know is how to handle the woman. How to get her to shut up for long enough for her to listen to what one wants to say or ask. How to influence her.'

True to what he was beginning to recognise as her form, Sally swooped on the final—and least important-question.

'Influence her? You mean, as in flowers, chocolates, or other offerings?' She shook her head decisively, and if the glossy brown hair bounced, Grant only noticed it incidentally. Or so he told himself.

'Doesn't work!' Sally continued. 'She's incorruptible, our Flo. One of the gynae men once tried everything he knew— talk about bribery and corruption! He even offered a free hysterectomy for Flo's mother. Then he ended up with an hour a week less operating time, rather than the full four-hour session he'd been after.'

'A free hysterectomy for her mother?' Grant found the words echoing hollowly from his lips.

Sally nodded.

'It's true. But to get back to theatre usage, the problem is largely a nursing one. I mean, mere doctors do their rostered hours plus overtime as a matter of course. Junior doctors on staff don't even start to count overtime until they've done seventy hours, and even if they can find time to claim it, Admin always argues.'

She flashed a grin at Grant.

'We're not unionised well enough,' she told him. 'Nurses, now, they're different. Come four-thirty when their theatre shift ends, they go automatically onto overtime, and Admin hates paying it. Upsets the budget. It doesn't matter that a morning session went an hour over its schedule, as long as the afternoon's ops end on time. It's a known fact that surgical residents in specialties who have afternoon sessions sew faster than ones who only work mornings.'

Grant had to laugh.

'Oh, dear,' he managed when he'd finally controlled himself, 'I know there's an element of truth in all of that, but the image of afternoon surgeons sewing furiously, one eye on the clock, was too much for me.'

Sally smiled, pleased she'd been able to amuse him. Though amusement hadn't been a priority. All she'd been trying to do had been to divert him away from the subject of mixed changing rooms.

A diversion she intended to continue.

'I might have exaggerated slightly, but that's the basic concept. Operating hours are eight-thirty to four-thirty, full stop. Of course, we have the minor procedures theatres attached to A and E, to the ICU and Paediatrics, plus two theatres staffed for emergencies around the clock. But nursing staff on those are rostered on duty rather than on call, and if there's nothing happening in Theatre, they float.'

Judging by his acceptance of the word, Grant understood about floaters, although the sudden switch from smiling man to one who looked desperately worried puzzled her.

'Floaters aren't that bad,' she said, hoping to tease him into more laughter—or at least banish the worry.

He glanced across the table at her, met her eyes and smiled.

Not a laugh but almost as good.

'I'm sorry,' he said. 'I hadn't heard the expression before but the nurse who found my brother was a "floater" between Theatre and the ICU. Sam explained the meaning.'

'Sam Abbot? Sam Abbot found your brother?'

Now the man looked wary.

'You know Sam?'

Sally beamed at him.

'Of course. As well as working together in Theatre for ages, she's a distant cousin. Not that we ever saw much of each other until she began nursing. She grew up in the country.'

Hmm. That didn't help. Rather than looking less wary, he was now looking downright dubious.

'I suppose—' He broke off, frowned, then spoke again, either rephrasing what he'd been about to say or changing the subject. 'Does she often go off on her own?'

'Bush-walking? All the time?' The penny dropped. 'You mean she *literally* found your brother? In the bush? What was he doing there? How did he get lost?'

Grant ran a hand through his short dark hair, and studied the woman across the table from him. She'd now spooned half the tub of yoghurt over half the fruit and was packing the remainder of the fruit into the space in the tub, not missing a beat in the conversation as she continued to organise their shared meal.

'We're still piecing that together,' he replied, nodding his thanks as she passed the plate across to him and stabbed a slice of rockmelon with her fork.

'He said he couldn't remember a lot of things. Amnesia? You must be worried. Is he really a doctor?'

The disbelief in the last question was so evident that Grant chuckled.

'Trained and tested.' He was doing what she'd done earlier, answering the last question first.

Although he fully intended answering the other questions, not evading them as Sally had managed.

'Yes, he had a knock on the head and suffered some amnesia, although apparently it was more severe a day or two ago. And, yes, I'm very worried. Any head injury is serious, and one resulting in the level of amnesia he's had is doubly so.'

'Do you want me to arrange a scan—I mean, you can arrange it but do it in my name if you like. Because of not treating relatives.'

He heard a slight echo of uncertainty in her usually determined voice, but guessed it wasn't to do with offering her services. Maybe she had as little desire to become better acquainted, out of work time, with him as he did with her.

Of course, his avoidance tactics were necessary—given the attraction he was feeling towards her and his experience of where a relationship could lead.

But why would she be wary?

Perhaps her boyfriend, partner, husband—no, he knew she wasn't married—wouldn't like it.

'I'd love you to arrange a scan,' Grant told her, 'but he tells me he's perfectly all right and I can't force the man to do something he doesn't want to do.'

'Have you tried blackmail?' the pretty-faced senior resident said calmly. 'I can almost always blackmail my brothers into doing what I want them to do.'

Sex, drugs and rock and roll! The phrase Miss Flintock had used in conjunction with Dr Cochrane's brothers flitted through Grant's head.

'Only "almost" always?' he queried, and she smiled at him, her delight lighting not only the gold lights in her eyes but her entire face so she seemed to radiate fun in the same way the sun shared its heat around.

'Sometimes I have to resort to violence,' she whispered, 'but I try to keep that quiet.'

And what you're doing, smiling at her silly conversation, I don't know, common sense muttered, but an empty feeling, deep in Grant's gut, suggested that it was too late for common sense. Something about this woman had sneaked beneath his defences.

He stared out across the huge room, and tried to remember that other cafeteria where he'd sat with Erica. Tried to recall the pain he'd felt when she'd told him she was marrying Lance. Because he'd be better for her career, she'd said, delivering that final blow with a smile that had suggested he'd understand—that *he*, Grant, was career-focussed enough for it to seem as reasonable to him as it apparently had been to her.

But the worst of it had been the gossip. The fact that everyone in the hospital had seemed to know what had happened. Before it had happened? Had they known all along? After all, there must have been some courtship before Lance Binstead had proposed.

These were the questions that had haunted Grant for months afterwards, when he'd also had to cope with the pitying looks cast his way, and the offers of consolation from female colleagues.

'I guess it's a lesson for both of us,' he'd said to Tom when they'd escaped for a rare weekend together and had been rediscovering the joy of a couple of days of surf, sun and sand. 'Not to get emotionally involved with colleagues. With anyone for that matter, but especially not with colleagues. We either take the love-'em-and-leave-'em approach or steer clear of women altogether, at least until we're ready to settle down.'

And at the time, Tom agreed.

'That's where someone like Jocelyn will come in handy,' he said, with all the arrogance of young manhood. 'Someone sensible who'll make an excellent wife, home-maker and mother. Run the house, entertain guests and not expect all the flowery stuff that women in love seem to crave.'

'Perhaps we could clone her,' Grant replied. And they laughed together and toasted their 'sensible' futures.

But the memory of his pain, of the hurt Erica's behaviour and the ensuing talk caused, remained, and he, at least, stuck to his determination to not get too emotionally involved with the women with whom he worked.

A decision that had been strengthened by circumstances later in his career, he reminded himself grimly, thinking of the two bright young lives lost to the world through a work relationship that had gone horribly wrong. He pushed back his chair, and stood up. Never again, he'd vowed. Never again!

'Thank you for sharing your lunch with me,' he said, looking down at the table in case startled brown eyes should weaken his resolution. 'I'll have to do the same for you one day.'

It was only as he strode purposefully out the door that he realised he hadn't got onto the subject he'd wanted to discuss—the changing rooms.

Or had he been skilfully diverted away from it?

Sally watched the door swing shut behind Grant's broad straight back and heaved a sigh of relief. Somehow they'd managed to avoid the changing-room question—but for how long could she use diversionary tactics before he became suspicious?

She looked down at the remnants of their lunch. He hadn't eaten the apple. In fact, he hadn't finished his fruit and yoghurt.

Perhaps he didn't like yoghurt.

Though he *had* left very suddenly. What had they been talking about? Could she have upset him in some way?

She sighed again, but relief didn't get a look-in this time.

'Problems?'

Jerry settled into a vacant chair and she smiled at him.

'Why would you think that?' she asked.

'That sigh came from somewhere down in your boots,' he said. 'And I've been watching. The boss left in a hurry. One minute, the two of you are sitting here, all pally, laughing and joking, and the next he's up and out of here faster than a man who's sat on an ants' nest.'

'I think I'm doomed to upset him,' Sally admitted. 'Though what it was this time, I've no idea. Threatening violence to my brothers? Could that have bothered him? I'm sure that's all we were talking about, but he makes me so nervous I tend to rattle on a bit.'

'He shouldn't make you nervous,' Jerry assured her. 'You're a top surgeon, you're practically a genius, if your exam results are any guide, and you're a darned hard worker. What more could any department head want on his team?'

What more, indeed?

The reason they'd lunched together flashed through Sally's head.

'A man, that's what more he could want!' she said gloomily. 'He's against the mixed changing rooms. He must be one of those throwbacks to the Dark Ages who believe surgery's not for women. Perhaps he's enough of a Neanderthal to still believe a woman's place is in the kitchen.'

'I'll tell him you said that,' Jerry teased, and Sally glanced anxiously around.

'No need to tell him. He probably heard. Sometimes I wonder if he's got me wired for sound, the things he does happen to overhear.'

'You've only a year to go,' Jerry reminded her.

'Do you think I don't keep telling myself that?' she replied. 'It's like a mantra sounding in my head. One year to go. One year to go!'

She smiled at her colleague.

'And speaking of going, I should be off. His lordship's lecturing so I'll whip up to the ward office and struggle through some paperwork.'

'Good luck with it,' Jerry said. 'I'm actually going to sit in on his lecture. He's good, Sally!'

'I know that,' she agreed. ' Darned good!'

And darned attractive, darned sexy, and darned well doing damage to her usually impervious heart!

Maybe the bookwork would act as an antidote!

She was still struggling with forms and figures at five-thirty when Jerry poked his head through the door to wish her goodnight. Minutes later, footsteps in the corridor slowed then another head poked around the jamb.

A very dark, sleekly attractive female head.

'I'm looking for Dr Hudson,' the woman said, coming into view and revealing an elegantly tailored skirt and jacket outfit that made Sally ache to be taller. 'Someone told me he might be here.'

Sally looked around the small space designated to doctors on the neuro ward.

'Nope, he's definitely not here,' she said, deliberately casual as an irrational urge to snarl at the woman all but swamped her.

'I can see that,' her visitor snapped. 'I want to know where he is.'

Sally shrugged.

'We don't keep tabs on each other, you know. I assume you've tried phoning or paging him.'

'He's not in his office so phoning there's not much use, and he's not answering his mobile.'

A placatory smile now replaced the slightly petulant look on the woman's face.

'Could you page him for me?'

Sally shook her head.

'If I page him he'll assume he's needed up here on the ward, which he isn't,' she said, while inwardly telling herself it was cheap to feel some satisfaction.

The smile thinned but remained in place as the woman stepped closer.

'I know I'm being a nuisance,' she said. 'Especially when you're so busy.' She waved a languid hand towards the piles of paperwork. 'I'm a trained nurse myself so I know what it's like, but Grant, Dr Hudson… '

The smile became coy.

'It's not public knowledge. Not something he wanted discussed within a new work situation, but—' Coy shifted to conspiratorial '—if I say I've just moved up from Sydney, taken a new job at far less pay, you'd understand, wouldn't you?'

Understand you and Grant Hudson as an item? Not in a million years! Sally thought.

But was all her irritation the result of the woman's manner? Or did it stem from the slightly sick feeling in the pit of her stomach?

'Whoever you are, I still can't page him to come to the ward under false pretences. If you tell me your name, I could page him and leave a message for him to phone you.'

'I've already done that,' the still unnamed woman snarled, all pretence of niceness gone. 'And he hasn't answered. All right for him to leave cryptic messages about Tom being found, but has he followed it up? Or made arrangements for dinner when he's stood me up the last two nights?'

She spun around and stormed from the room, her high heels clacking down the corridor as she headed for the lift.

Sally waited until the echo died away, then she pushed aside the closest papers, folded her arms on the desk and rested her head on them.

Professional colleagues, that's all we are, she reminded herself. The man's private life is none of your business.

And at your age, it's hardly surprising your suppressed hormones would start twitching back to life. Someone had to be the catalyst.

'Sleeping on the job, Dr Cochrane?'

The voice made her shoulders stiffen. Had she developed extrasensory powers—an ability to call him up, make him materialise, merely by thinking of him?

She debated pretending to be asleep. Remaining exactly where she was, head hidden from view. Decided it wasn't an option. Apart from anything else, her hormonal twitches might show! She slowly raised her head.

'There was a woman looking for you. She went that-a-way.'

Sally jerked her thumb towards the corridor, and pulled the pile of papers back to the front of the desk.

'A woman?'

He sounded puzzled enough for Sally's sense of humour to return. She waved her hands in the air to indicate a female form.

'A shapely human, supposedly fashioned from Adam's rib,' she said helpfully. 'The gender you object to in the changing rooms. Ringing any bells?'

Blue eyes grew murderous.

'I know exactly what you meant by woman, Dr Cochrane,' he muttered. 'I was after a little more elucidation. Females of the species are in the majority in hospitals so something more definitive than ''a woman'' might have helped.'

The pompous tone tightened Sally's nerves another notch, but she wasn't going to let him see that. Smiling impishly, she tilted her head to one side and said, 'Five-nine, brunette, tailored suit and blood-red talons? Claims to be a *special* person in your life? Ringing any bells?'

She rather fancied a faint flush of colour rose beneath his cheeks but from the glow in his eyes it could have been rage. However, he held himself together remarkably well, and counter-attacked, saying, 'Showing talons of your own, Doctor?' Sally had to concede him a point.

She relaxed enough to grin at him. 'Only small ones,' she assured him. 'Must be hunger getting to me. After all, I only ate half my lunch.'

Grant Hudson threw his arms into the air in a gesture of surrender, and laughed loudly.

'You win,' he told her, when he'd caught his breath. 'I can't possibly counter that one. Tell me, are you always this combative or do I merit special treatment?' He paused, but before she could consider a reply he added, 'And is it as a man, or as your boss, I'm singled out?'

'That's at least two and possibly three questions,' Sally

told him, rustling frantically through the papers in the hope she'd give an impression of furious busyness. And he'd take the hint and go away.

'None of which you're going to answer,' he suggested smoothly. And far from going away, he settled one hip comfortably on the opposite side of the desk and gave every indication of staying for ever.

In fact, he reached out and lifted one of her bits of paper, then pretended to study it as he said, 'It's an almost an art form with you, isn't it? Dodging questions.'

Sally shrugged, which he could take as a yes if he wanted. 'I really do have work to do, and your friend was anxious to contact you, so perhaps you should be looking for her rather than bothering me.'

'Am I bothering you, Sally?'

Something in the way he asked the question made her stomach curl, and she looked up to meet his eyes. They didn't give the slightest clue as to what he was thinking. Nothing there but the query itself, as if the question were as basic as one about a patient's pulse or blood pressure.

'Of course you're bothering me,' she said crossly, and let the truth have a moment to itself before she added, 'Taking up room on the desk, messing up my papers, picking things up and putting them back in the wrong pile.'

His sigh had a hint of disappointment in it—or was that wishful thinking on her part? But whatever it meant, her protest had worked for he stood up and reached across the desk to replace the paper he'd been holding.

'See! Back in the right place!' he said, then he walked out of the room, leaving Sally feeling curiously bereft.

Finding Tom was one thing, Grant decided savagely. But coping with the emotional fallout was more than a man should have to handle while struggling to settle into a new job.

A task not simplified by a snippy, sniping resident who never gave a straight answer to his questions, fluttered long dark eyelashes over her gold-flecked eyes and deliberately flaunted her near-naked body in the changing rooms!

Well, perhaps not deliberately. He grudgingly gave Sally the benefit of that particular doubt as he headed back towards his office, hoping to track Jocelyn down before she took it into her head to go to his home.

Where she'd find Tom and, no doubt, be told, too bluntly, truths she didn't want to hear.

He stopped mid-stride, backtracked to a phone and dialled his home number.

'Have you been there all along?' he demanded, when his brother answered.

'No, I've just got in,' Tom told him cheerfully. 'Sean, one of Sam's brothers, took me shopping. You haven't improved as far as stocking your cupboards are concerned.'

'You shopped?' Concern fought with disbelief, and the latter won. 'What with? You've got no money, no cards.'

He heard his brother's familiar chuckle echo down the line.

'Worried I'm living off borrowed funds? I phoned my bank this morning, explained the situation and was able to withdraw some cash from the local branch by this afternoon.'

'I should have left you some money,' Grant muttered, concerned he could have forgotten something so basic.

'Hey, relax! How many times do I have to tell you you're not your brother's keeper?'

'No?' Grant said, but he smiled as he spoke. He knew his arrival in the world twenty minutes before Tom shouldn't have resulted in such an over-developed sense of responsibility, but he was unable to curb it. 'Well, in that case, I'll leave you to deal with Jocelyn. She's been looking for me here, but as we missed each other, I guess she'll head over there. I know you told her before you went away that there was no future for the two of you together but, as we both know, she's not a woman who listens to what she's told. She should be ringing the bell any minute.'

Tom's groan made him chuckle.

'Good thing I'm not your keeper, eh?' Grant said, and hung up.

Then, although he'd had the last laugh, he felt a sense of disloyalty. After all, Tom would never have drifted into his relationship with Jocelyn if she hadn't been so upset when he, Grant, had begun seeing Erica all those years ago.

So where did that leave him? Was it his turn to take on the role of comforter?

Clearly, that's how Jocelyn saw it. But, unfortunately, as she had when he'd defected and she'd turned to Tom, she wanted more than comforting. She wanted permanence. Stability.

Marriage?

He shuddered, then groaned aloud, startling a young nurse waiting for the same lift.

'Bad day?' she said, smiling sympathetically.

'You don't know the half of it!' he told her.

CHAPTER FIVE

By FRIDAY, Sally was resigned to the fact that her hormones were in a tangle over Grant Hudson—and was becoming adept at avoidance tactics so her overly responsive nerve endings didn't get too much chance to react.

Not that avoiding him was difficult. In fact, if she'd had a suspicious nature, she'd have suspected he was doing the same thing.

But the stress of keeping out of his way was beginning to tell, and by late afternoon she'd completed the 'can't wait' reports and was hurrying up to the ward to do a final round, eager to get away. Looking forward to two days entirely free from all thoughts of work.

'I was wondering if you'd be free any time over the weekend to discuss a few matters.'

He'd not only crept up behind her but he'd stolen some of her words! She spun to face him.

'What kind of matters?' she demanded, then felt her cheeks heat as she heard the echo of her aggression in the words.

One raised eyebrow told her he'd also heard it, but his tone, when he answered, was mild.

'The splitting of the team for one thing,' he said, and the hint of a smile played around his lips. 'I think it was your suggestion, wasn't it?'

Think work, not smiles, she told herself. Splitting the team could mean two registrars would be appointed. A possible job opportunity for next year, right here in the hospital she knew and loved.

But she was still suspicious.

'Why talk to me, not Daniel?'

The smile was swallowed by a sigh. Which was a good thing, really.

'Daniel has been in this hospital for exactly three months longer than I have. I shall, of course, consult him, and have, in fact, spoken to him about it, but it is you who have the experience of how things work here.'

He paused then added, 'It's the benefit of that experience, I want, Dr Cochrane, nothing else.'

Sally guessed at what the 'nothing else' implied and hoped the embarrassment she was feeling wasn't obvious.

'I suppose I can make time,' she said, grouching out the words so he didn't think she was eager. Or too excited about the idea—which went a step further than she'd suggested. 'In your office?'

Grant shrugged.

'Actually, I was looking forward to getting away from the place for a couple of days. My unit has a great view, and I've a coffee-maker and plenty of beans.'

He hesitated, and if she hadn't seen his decisiveness in action she'd have thought he was uncertain.

'I'll do a quick ward round early Saturday morning,' he continued, 'but, barring emergencies, I should be home by nine-thirty. Would ten suit you? Is Saturday OK? I should have asked that first.'

Definitely uncertain.

But rather than ponder the question of why, she decided to take the initiative—and the decisiveness.

'Ten on Saturday. Your unit. No worries.'

She swung away from him, then realised, as he fell in beside her, that he was also heading for the ward.

'You're far more conscientious than Ted ever was,' she told him, more to break the silence than to compliment him. 'He did teaching rounds and visited pet patients, but rarely just popped in like you're doing now.'

He grinned at her.

'And like you're doing now!' he reminded her. 'For me, it's an excuse. I dislike the "business" of running a unit and, much as I tell myself it's necessary to have data to show the cost efficiency and staff ratios and all the other info the number-crunchers want, I tend to use a visit to the wards to escape it all.'

'A very temporary escape,' Sally reminded him, nodding to thank him for opening the door for her. 'The data still has to be collated, the numbers crunched.'

'Which is why I'm staying back tonight,' he said. 'Virtuous, aren't I?'

His eyes invited her to share the joke but her head knew sharing jokes with this man was a dangerous occupation. Akin to entering a lion's den, the way her heart was behaving.

Counter-attack—that's what was needed here.

'And what does the brunette think about you working such long hours?'

She saw the laughter fade from his face and for a moment regretted her impertinent question.

But self-preservation was important, too, she reminded herself.

'I don't think that's any of your business, Dr Cochrane,' Grant said crisply, then he turned away, bestowing his smiles like blessings on two women at the nurses' station—shutting her out in the cold.

Which was where she deserved to be. And should want to be, if she had any common sense at all!

Having parted so badly, it took all Sally's strength of will to press the button which would announce her arrival at Grant's unit block the following morning.

But the ogre within greeted her quite calmly, reminding

her of his floor number, then having the door open in welcome when she exited the lift.

'Good morning.'

The formal greeting, pleasantly uttered, should have been easy to acknowledge, but for Sally, the sight of him—a casual version of her new boss—dried her lips and paralysed her tongue.

She made do with a nod, and followed him inside, telling herself it was normal for a man spending the day at home to be attired in faded denim shorts and casual shoes.

The fact that the visible section of the legs between shorts and shoes were long, strong, tanned and lightly dusted with silky dark hair shouldn't be affecting her speech patterns. Any more than an ordinary cotton-knit shirt that clung too lovingly to a well-sculpted chest should be drying her lips.

Hormonal—that's all it was.

But how to damp them down again—those now-rampaging endocrine secretions?

Grant was indicating for her to sit, asking how she liked her coffee, and somehow she managed to both reply and move, though she did slump a trifle too gratefully into the soft leather armchair.

By the time he returned, a tray with two steaming mugs and a plate of biscuits balanced in his hands, she'd recovered sufficiently to be able to thank him.

He set her coffee on the table in front of her, put the biscuits between them and took a chair facing towards her.

'Most people comment on the view,' he said, nodding his head towards the wall of floor-to-ceiling glass that offered the city like a three-dimensional photo to anyone walking into the room.

Sally was about to admit she hadn't noticed it when she realised that would be a gross tactical error. After all, what else could she possibly have been noticing?

His legs?

The groan almost escaped but she bit it back and made the appropriate nice-view noises.

'But, of course, you'd seen it before,' Grant said. 'On your mission of mercy.'

'Mission of mercy?'

This time the involuntary sounds did escape. She was behaving as if she were half-witted.

'Coming to see if I lay dead on the bathroom tiles.'

His smile told her he'd put two and two together to make a creditable four, but smiles were to be avoided at all costs.

'That time I didn't get beyond the door,' she told him. 'Now, what are your thoughts on splitting the team?'

If he was disappointed she'd switched so determinedly to work-related matters, he didn't show it, launching smoothly into his preliminary ideas on the subject.

'Of course, I haven't been here long enough for my opinions to carry much weight with the board, so I'll need to tread carefully, but if we can collate patient numbers, the length of the elective waiting list, comparisons with other hospitals, and have something prepared, then in a couple of months I can start planting the seeds of the idea.'

'You'll hit a brick wall with theatre usage,' Sally told him, pleased to have a real problem to distract her. 'That's where the bottleneck occurs in all surgical specialties.'

'What about day surgery? So many of our procedures could be done in that way.'

'It's a trend that's growing,' Sally agreed, 'and becoming more acceptable to the patients. But we're way down the list as far as operating time in the day theatres. The eye people got into the swing of it first. It's not so long since a cataract op meant three days in hospital, now they do dozens an hour.'

'Dozens?' Grant said dryly, and Sally had to smile.

'Plenty,' she amended. 'And the plastic chaps are in on the act, not to mention the orthopods with their minor surgery and arthroscopy. Because they've already established their claims on the facilities, it's hard for us to force the issue of extra time allotment there.'

'Hard, but not impossible?' Grant mused, and Sally, watching his face and reading the strength and determination in it, wondered if he considered anything impossible.

He switched the conversation back to patient numbers, asked about the other public and major private hospitals in the city and how much cross-fertilisation there was between them.

'We work well together,' Sally said. 'Only two of the others have neuro wards, so we get referrals. Don't be surprised if your pain patients increase. They're not everybody's favourite people.'

His wry chuckle rippled in the air, its effect skipping down Sally's spine like playful fingers. She shifted her shoulders to remove the resulting goose bumps, and missed his question.

Something about specialising?

Herself?

'I haven't decided,' she said, praying she'd guessed correctly. 'My main focus has been on this year—getting through the exams, and claiming my qualifications. I've already put in the time required.'

He leaned forward, his elbows on his knees, and looked into her eyes.

'I was going to ask you about that. I know from your file you spent four months in Chicago, but that was two years ago and the time there counted. So how come you didn't sit your final exams last year?'

Sally was surprised that the question, which usually caused such pain, today provoked nothing more than a wave of sadness.

'I took some time off,' she said, then, seeing sufficient

determination in his eyes to suggest he wasn't going to accept that answer, she added, 'For personal reasons.'

Which were either bad or sad, or perhaps both, Grant decided, as the brown eyes grew cloudy and the golden lights dimmed.

He wasn't insensitive enough to push her further, but he'd have liked to have known more. Would have liked her to have felt she could talk to him about it.

'So will you head overseas, go into private practice or try for a job at another hospital when you finish this year?'

She half smiled.

'If you can wangle a second team, maybe staying on would be an option. If we could get two registrars' positions... Or wouldn't you want me?'

A simple question, but the response it triggered in his body was nothing short of bizarre. After all, he was the one who'd made the 'rule' about not getting too involved socially.

A rule he knew made sense!

And she had all her clothes on today.

'I'm not getting sucked into that conversation,' he said, congratulating himself on sounding so rational. 'Before I know it, you'll be after my job.'

She shook her head.

'Not yet,' she told him, a teasing little smile flirting about her lips and returning the glow to the gold flecks in her eyes. 'Not enough experience. But give me time. You'll move on to greener pastures, and then it will be my turn.'

Her certainty intrigued him.

'No wish for greener pastures yourself?'

She shook her head.

'Been there and done that,' she told him. 'I enjoy travel, and won't say no if opportunities to attend conferences arise, but Brisbane's my home and I'm here to stay.'

More than intriguing, it was downright puzzling that she should be so definite.

'What about family? Getting married? Having kids? There are times when department heads have lives as busy as first-year interns. Hard to fit in family responsibilities.'

She glared at him.

'Men seem to manage it,' she reminded him, and he grinned.

'That's because most of them have a good woman behind them.'

He thought of Erica, and smiled to himself. Lance Binstead had already been well established by the time he'd cast aside one wife and settled for a younger model. But if he'd expected to have a 'good woman behind him' he'd have been in for a shock. Erica's focus had been wholly and solely on her career. On breaking the glass ceiling that stopped many women's careers.

Erica!

He said the word experimentally in his head but felt no pain. No stab of regret, no crushing load of angst.

'Perhaps I'm cured,' he muttered. He only realised he'd spoken aloud when Sally asked, 'Cured of what?'

He grinned at her. 'Would you believe, cured of love?' he challenged. 'Or the fall-out it can leave behind?'

'Not for an instant,' she retorted. 'I imagine you're far too strong a character to let an irrational emotion like love cause you a moment's angst.'

'Speaking from experience, Dr Cochrane?' he countered, surprised that so attractive a woman would speak so slightingly of love.

But her answering chuckle was even more surprising.

'Not of love,' she assured him. 'Lust maybe, but so long ago any angst that might have existed is well and truly forgotten.'

He studied her, suddenly uncertain about how this conversation had started—or where it was leading! Yet he couldn't let it drop.

'You don't class lust as an irrational emotion?'

Her wide smile pressed an almost dimple into her left cheek. A tiny indentation like a shadow of itself.

'I class lust as over-active hormones,' Sally said firmly. 'After all, we've been genetically programmed to seek pleasure in sex to ensure the survival of the species. Certain triggers release the necessary flow of endorphins which make us feel good. Purely physiological, Doctor. Now, shall we get back to splitting the team? Perhaps list any information it might be useful to have, and where to source it? Consider a partial split within the existing team?'

'Pre-empting a decision?' Grant teased, following her lead back to work-related topics but wanting to keep the camaraderie he felt between them.

'Merely smoothing the way for a possible transition,' she said, but the gold lights danced in her eyes and he couldn't help but smile at her.

Purely physiological, he reminded himself!

However, they did get down to work, discussing the possible or probable consequences of roster variations and trying to foretell the benefits of a split-team approach.

Ideas sparked between them, and they strayed into other work-related areas, Grant enjoying the challenges her quick mind threw his way, revelling in the opportunity to explore different avenues which might lead to more efficient use of resources and therefore better patient outcomes.

So when his visitor glanced at her watch and gave a small gasp of surprise, he was disappointed.

'I've kept you so long—why not stay to lunch? I'd usually be hesitant to offer, but Tom stocked the cupboards and refrigerator before he went back to Sydney, so at least let me feed you.'

But Sally was on her feet, and looking flustered enough for him to suspect she was already running late for something far more important than lunch with her boss.

'I can't, it's after one and it's my turn to shop. I should have found time during the week, but things happened. The boys will be dragging their bodies out of bed and prowling the kitchen in search of sustenance. They'll eat the furniture if I don't get there soon.'

'The boys?' Grant echoed, and she shot him a smile so full of warmth it was like a small personal sun, shining just for him.

'My brothers,' she said simply. 'Three of them. Brad, Phil and Eddie. Not really boys any more. They're grown men. And not known for early rising, but any time after midday their stomachs rouse them. I'll have to grab something at the local shops and throw it through the door, then get on with the serious business of filling a trolley or two.'

He chuckled at the image, although he was certain she was joking.

'You make it sound like feeding time at the zoo.'

The smile returned.

'You've got the picture!' she said, fumbling in her handbag, presumably for keys.

And, having found them, she hesitated, looking at Grant, her brown eyes studying him with an indefinable uncertainty. Then she gave a little nod—decision made—and said, 'I've enjoyed this morning, although it was nothing more than shop-talk. Exciting, really—projecting the future.'

Sally nodded again, and the shiny brown cap of hair moved slightly, so a stray ray of sun caught the red-gold gleams among the soft strands.

'It was fun!'

She was so serious, he had to smile.

'You sound surprised that talking shop, as you call it, could be fun!'

She gave a little huff of laughter, and the smile grew warmer.

'I guess I was. Perhaps because most of our discussions at

work are, necessarily, patient orientated, rather than work orientated. Or—'

She stopped abruptly and Grant saw a faint wash of colour
in her cheeks.

Or what? Grant wondered, as he followed her hasty move
towards the front door.

Had she been about to add something personal?

Something to do with the company making the discussion
more pleasant?

Don't kid yourself, buster! He escorted her to the lift, summoned it and waited until it arrived, intrigued by this woman
of whom he knew so little.

Intrigued by *and* attracted to?

No way. Bad enough to have Tom imagining himself in
love with a woman he'd known less than a week. And
women on the team were off limits, remember!

But when the lift arrived to whisk her downwards he found
himself joining her in the metal cubicle.

'I'll see you to your car,' he said, responding to her glance
of surprised enquiry.

Then, in case it sounded too intrusive, he added, 'Check
my mail.'

'Of course,' she said, lips twitching with amusement.

Duh! It was Saturday. No mail. Was he ever making a fool
of himself.

And it wasn't even spring.

Could it be Tom's fault? Could they now be doing the
twin thing with hormonal urges?

Surely not. Attraction wasn't like pain. Not something he
was likely to feel because Tom was suffering, like the headache and bad ankle which had plagued him for days when
Tom had been missing.

But seeing Sally to her car gave him new food for thought.
A distraction.

The vehicle looked more like a fifth-hand student-mobile

than something a well-paid fourth-year resident should be driving.

Not that it was any of his business, he reminded himself, listening to the missing beat in the engine and the grumble of an exhaust in need of more than patching.

He watched it trundle through the security bar at the entrance to the car park, and for some reason one of Miss Flintock's more obscure remarks now echoed in his head.

Sex, drugs and rock and roll. A phrase used in conjunction with Sally Cochrane's brothers.

And they woke up ravenously hungry.

Wasn't ravenous hunger a byproduct of drug-taking?

He found himself more puzzled than intrigued—more uncomfortable, in fact—as he made his way back to his apartment. No! No one in their right mind could associate someone as vibrantly, obviously, shiningly healthy as Sally Cochrane with drugs.

Not that he was in his right mind, he'd decided by Monday, when the drive to work was enlivened by the thought of seeing Sally again, and his heart was coming menacingly close to skittering with excitement.

'You don't get involved with women on your team,' he reminded himself.

Especially not women who attracted trouble like a magnet attracted iron filings, he amended later, walking into the neuro ward tearoom to find his registrar and fourth-year resident arguing loudly.

'Your voices are carrying through to the ward,' he said, hoping the cold sobriety of his voice might cool them both down.

But while Daniel stopped immediately, and walked away, heading for the urn and messing with coffee-mugs, Sally, her cheeks flushed red with fury, was too wound up to listen to common sense. She swung towards Grant to continue the attack.

'You said we could keep her. Said to run non-expensive tests. I've listed her in another three nursing homes in the area where she's always lived, and what does he do? Sends her home.'

She flung her arms in the air and spun away, as if her fury demanded the release of movement.

Grant struggled for a moment. The conversation was certainly ringing bells. But which bells?

'Miss Wingate?' he asked Daniel, as Sally had stomped to the far end of the room and was glaring out the window.

Daniel nodded.

'A neighbour called in to see her this morning and found her unconscious. An assortment of tablets was scattered across her bedside table. She's down in A and E and has had her stomach pumped but there'll be questions asked.'

'The ambulance-bearers brought the tablets in.' Sally left the window to offer this further information. 'From the lack of packaging—no empty blister packs, no bottles—in her house, it's possible she was secreting tablets while she was in here,' she added, and Grant could hear the distress of responsibility in her voice—see it in her eyes.

'Sally's off on this blame thing,' Daniel interjected. 'But there's no proof Miss Wingate didn't take the drugs she was prescribed while she was a patient, and even if she didn't, is it our problem?'

'Of course it's our problem but that's not the point,' Sally snapped at him. 'We knew she dreaded going home and yet we sent her back there.'

'We can't keep patients indefinitely,' Grant said, playing arbiter, although the woman's act of desperation both saddened and angered him.

'I'm not talking about "patients" plural, but one woman.

A person, not the aneurysm in bed eight or the neuralgia in bed twelve.'

He understood exactly what she was saying, and how she felt, but Daniel had done nothing wrong—according to hospital protocol. And as he was in the right, he should be backed up in his decision.

'She's one patient, Dr Cochrane, one of many on our books,' Grant reminded the resident. 'We can't take ongoing responsibility for each and every individual we treat.'

'No?' Sally shot the word at him then flung out of the room.

'Has Miss Wingate been readmitted?' Grant asked Daniel.

The resident shrugged.

'I've no idea. As far as I know, we haven't been connected with it at all. And wouldn't have been only Sally came in early and found Miss Wingate had been discharged, phoned the house and got no answer so she phoned the neighbour, who was listed as a contact on the patient files.'

He glanced towards the door through which Sally had fled and added, 'Seems to me, if she'd let well alone, the woman might have got her wish to die.'

The seemingly callous words jolted Grant.

'You're saying Sally shouldn't have worried? That if Miss Wingate chose to suicide, she should have been allowed that choice?'

He must have sounded startled, for Daniel responded with an ingratiating smile.

'I don't disagree with voluntary euthanasia,' he said. 'In certain cases. Where a person makes an informed decision. Miss Wingate wasn't stupid or senile, and if she collected those tablets here, it was a predetermined act.'

'Of desperation!' Sally, who'd returned in time to hear this statement, said. 'She didn't want to die, she just didn't want to live alone!'

She shoved a slim file into Grant's hands.

'Anyway, she's not your worry now, Daniel. She's been admitted to the psych ward and maybe they'll be able to do more for her than we could.'

She turned to Grant and nodded at the file.

'That's a list of the drugs she was prescribed while she was our patient. In case someone asks.'

And with that she was gone again.

But meeting her later that night, up in the foyer to the psych ward, didn't surprise him. She was a tenacious little thing, this Sally Cochrane.

'How is she?' he asked, surmising Sally was on her way from a visit to Miss Wingate.

'Very upset at causing so much fuss.'

Grant looked for the golden lights in the eyes turned towards his, but her sadness over the woman's plight must have dimmed them.

'I was going to visit her. What do you think?'

She flashed him a smile—small lights returning.

'She's sleeping again now, but I think tomorrow she'd appreciate it.'

She glanced at her watch and added, 'But if you're just knocking off for the day, perhaps I could convey your greetings tomorrow. Ex-patient visits must be difficult to fit into your schedule.'

'And you're not still here?' he asked, enjoying an opportunity to tease her. 'What about your schedule?'

She flashed a smile.

'Residents don't have schedules,' she reminded him. 'Just waking hours and sleeping hours. Actually, I was on my way to the library and thought I'd call in to say hello. Rather a long hello!'

Grant checked his watch. Nine o'clock.

'Was she very distressed? Is that why you stayed so long?'

Slim shoulders rose and fell.

'Embarrassed more than distressed, but I told her it didn't

matter. That at least her actions had alerted people to the fact she needed help, and I assured her that being in the psych ward would prod the social work department into doing something for her.'

Grant found himself smiling.

'A rather extreme example of the squeaky wheel getting the oil?' he suggested.

Sally grinned at him.

'Exactly! In fact, when I spoke to the charge nurse, he said they'd already been advised that someone from the social work department will be here to take Miss Wingate on a tour of possible nursing homes. She has enough money, even without selling her house, to buy into hostel-type accommodation within a nursing home complex, but she hadn't known where to start organising it for herself.'

'You have been busy,' Grant said and saw from the way her eyes avoided his that he'd hit the nail on the head. Far from listening to his advice about not being responsible for the ongoing welfare of all their patients, Sally had gone right ahead, arranging things for the elderly woman.

He admired her for it but knew the pitfalls.

'You'll suffer burn-out far more quickly if you take on too much,' he warned her. 'I know it's hard, but if you can avoid getting emotionally involved with patients, your life will be easier.'

She looked directly at him now, and the gold lights were back, dancing in her eyes as she said, 'Yes, sure! This from a man who spent an hour last night working with Craig Greenway on the exercises the physio had suggested might improve the slight movement in his left hand.'

Grant tried desperately to ignore those dancing lights, but in the end he had to smile.

'OK, you've got me there. But that's no reason for you not to take my advice. Haven't you heard of "do what I say, not do what I do"?'

She smiled back at him.

'Personally, I'd rather it was the other way around. In fact, it was the one thing that warmed me to your appointment. Everything I heard about you suggested you were a hands-on administrator, a department head who actually liked being part of the department, not some figurehead and administrator way above it.'

He should have been pleased by this faint praise from his critical resident but something early in the words had jarred.

'The *one* thing that warmed you, Dr Cochrane? Did I have so many strikes against me?'

She shifted uncomfortably, looked at him and then away. Not at all good for his ego, this woman!

So why the attraction?

'No! That was wrong of me to say that. And Ted was a hands-on department head a long time ago, so I shouldn't have implied he wasn't.'

She looked back, directly into his eyes, as if she'd decided honesty was best. Grant braced himself for a few home truths.

'Patrick Miller applied as well. I worked under Patrick when he was neuro registrar and I was a first-year resident. Before that, in fact, during my internship.'

'Better the devil you know than the devil you don't?' Grant suggested, and won a smile. He felt strangely relieved her interest in the appointment had been for another applicant, not against him in particular.

'Exactly,' she said. 'I knew he wanted the job very badly, so I guess I was hoping he'd be appointed for his sake as well.' Her brow furrowed, and then, perhaps prompted by a need to have it all said, she added, 'But deep down I was pleased when your appointment was announced.'

'Yes?' Hope springs eternal! Surely now she'd say something nice.

'Of course,' she told him cheerfully. 'Think how much

better my CV will read with your name there as my department head. You're far better known in neuro circles.'

'Well, I'm glad I'm useful to you in some way!' he grumbled. 'Perhaps I can be helpful in other ways. Co-sign papers you're publishing or presenting, autograph your degree? Why stop at having me listed as department head on your CV? We might be able to go into business, selling positions through influence.'

She held up her hands.

'OK! It was a tactless thing to say, but you did ask,' she told him crossly. 'I'm sure I'll learn plenty from you as well. I was pleased for that reason as well.'

'But you'd rather have had Patrick Miller,' Grant muttered, although he had no idea why her attitude should be bugging him so much.

Sally scowled at the infuriating man. OK, so she'd started it, but why was he going on and on about the damn appointment?

'I didn't say I'd *rather* have Patrick Miller,' she reminded him, 'and this stupid conversation has gone on quite long enough. I don't know about you, but I'm starving. I'm going to forget the library and, as the boys will have eaten by now, I'm heading for the The Courtyard at Auchenflower for some pumpkin and ricotta ravioli which I intend washing down with a glass of good red.'

She'd thrown in her immediate plans as a gesture of defiance, not as an indication of where she'd be eating, so to see him walk into the casual eatery not ten minutes after she'd arrived was something of a shock.

'Someone in my apartment block had told me it was good,' he said by way of explanation. 'When you mentioned it, I realised how long it was since I'd eaten, and as the food fairies haven't restocked my cupboards since Tom left, it seemed the ideal time to try it.'

He gestured to the empty chair at her table.

'Keeping it for someone? May I join you? Or would you prefer to pretend we don't know each other and I'll sit across the other side of the room?'

'You're the man who made the no-fraternisation rule,' she reminded him. 'Actually, I was wrong when I said there was only one thing in your favour. That was another. The grapevine had it you didn't encourage personal relationships among your staff, and although that's a fairly antiquated notion in this day and age, I thought it might keep—make things easier.'

Grant listened to the words with disbelief.

'All I'm suggesting is sharing a table at a restaurant which is close to both our homes. That's hardly fraternisation, Dr Cochrane.'

'Well, in that case, you'd better sit down. Carole's waiting to take your order.'

She gestured towards a young waitress who was hovering uncertainly behind him.

He sat, and immediately regretted it. Regretted coming here in the first place. He bent his head over the menu and pretended to study it while he tried to sort through a mishmash of thoughts and emotions.

For a start, Sally's 'you'd better sit down' couldn't have been less welcoming, and, secondly, there was now another point she'd raised that was causing him inner concern. Her approval of the no-fraternisation rule.

There had been times, recently, when it had seemed to him as antiquated as she'd said it was, but that's because...

Well, it just was!

But unless he was mistaken, Sally's approval stemmed from something else.

Carole's cough reminded him of what he was supposed to be doing and he ordered a dish of seared salmon on mustard mash.

'Great choice,' Sally said, and for a moment Grant wondered if they should stick to food as a topic of conversation. Food, wine, restaurants in the area—there were any number of innocuous subjects. They could get through the meal without mentioning the hospital.

But would his brain let that happen?

No way!

Out popped the question he hadn't wanted to ask.

'It was a suggestion rather than a rule,' he pointed out, softening the approach. 'But tell me, why the Sally Cochrane endorsement of no fraternisation?'

She hesitated and he guessed. Guessed someone on the team had been bothering her.

Daniel?

Surely not. He was married. Not that a wedding ring stopped him flirting with the nurses. Someone bothering her would make the 'suggestion' appealing, Grant mused, and Daniel certainly had the ability to ruffle Sally's feathers.

Good thing the man wasn't here as Grant felt a sudden urge to punch his registrar on the nose.

'You're usually not so reticent,' he prompted, dousing the spurt of anger, but wanting to know more.

She grinned at him.

'It must be hunger. At the moment, that's taking precedent over all else, including the functioning of my brain. I can operate hungry—forget totally about food when I'm concentrating on what I'm doing—but think? Make decisions?' She shook her head. 'Never!'

He hid a smile. Sally did it well, this evasion or distraction tactic, and he guessed no matter how he worded the question, or how many times he asked, she'd avoid a direct answer.

And badly though he wanted to know, he admired her loyalty.

Yes, she had many admirable qualities, this woman with whom he was definitely not going to get involved!

CHAPTER SIX

THOUGH perhaps this time he wouldn't let Sally get away with the diversion! Grant waited until the food arrived and they'd eaten sufficient for hunger to be allayed. Then he resumed the conversation.

'So, now you've eaten, and can't use starvation as a diversionary tactic, are you going to expand on the subject of fraternisation? On why the suggestion earned me a tick of approval from you?' He tried a half-smile as he reminded her of her earlier words, hoping she'd take it as a casual remark, not the probe he intended it to be. 'Are you anti-fraternisation yourself?'

She glanced up and, as he caught the intent look in her eyes, he guessed she'd not been taken in.

'Determined, aren't you?' She spoke lightly and he bowed his head in reply.

'Seems I have to be to get a straight answer from you, Dr Cochrane.'

Her chuckle warmed the air between them and Grant found himself smiling for no particular reason.

And more determined than before to find out her feelings on the matter he was trying to discuss.

'Well?'

She studied him for a moment before she replied, leaning forward as if she needed to see him clearly when she spoke.

'I agree that, particularly with a small specialty, we can become too inwardly focussed—too obsessive about our own particular field. That's why—'

Sally realised what she'd been about to say and bit back the words about the changing rooms, and took a steadying breath. Not only did she have to deal with the contradictory reactions of caution and delight his presence caused, but she had also to avoid the pitfalls of his conversational challenges.

Without aggravating him unnecessarily!

'That's why?' he prompted.

'That's why it's best to mix with other people,' she said lamely, but knew he was too smart to believe that's what she'd intended saying. A new diversion was needed. 'Actually, it doesn't affect me at all, this no-fraternisation business. Fraternising with anyone is out of the question as far as I'm concerned. At least until I've finished my exams.'

'No social life at all?'

His eyebrow repeated the question.

'Is that so surprising?' Sally countered. 'Most specialists I know marry early so they don't have to be wasting time on a social life while they're studying, or marry later when their career's established.'

'Wasting time on a social life? That's a radical statement. Do I detect a touch of cynicism?'

Sally shrugged but then she smiled, enjoying the ebb and flow of the non-medical conversation.

Enjoying the company, though she knew she shouldn't be. This was a man to avoid, not someone with whom to discuss her non-existent social life.

She glanced up at him and knew from his eyes, and the alert way he held his head, that he was still waiting for an answer.

And would, no doubt, continue to wait.

'Probably!' she admitted. 'And it was also a generalisation, which I hate. But you must admit a lot of the mating-dating game is just that. A game. Or perhaps an elaborate dance, with set moves and counter moves. Even in the bird and animal kingdoms, there's a ritual to it all.'

'A game you've chosen not to play, or a dance to which you weren't invited?'

'Ouch! That's hitting a girl when she's down, that is.'

Then she thought about it.

'Chosen not to play,' she told him. 'At the moment. Until I'm through. Early on in my career, I came this close…' she held her thumb and forefinger millimetres apart '…to missing a scholarship and decided romance and study didn't mix.'

She'd finished her meal and was watching him as she spoke, so saw the shadows that darkened his eyes.

Emboldened by the ease between them, and possibly the relaxant effects of a pleasant cabernet, she said, 'You, too?'

The question startled Grant. What was she? A mind-reader? Someone who saw the past in his empty wineglass?

'Why would you ask?'

She smiled the little half-smile that seemed to flicker at one side of her lips before settling into place.

'Good guess?'

'Not really,' he said. 'Anyone my age and still single would be expected to have a few relationships in his past.'

'Only a few, Dr Hudson?' she teased, and he saw that silly smile playing around her lips again.

Not that he was going to be taken in by silly smiles. He finished the last morsels on his plate, then pushed it slightly back towards the centre of the table.

'That was delicious,' he said. 'If all the offerings are as good, I can understand the recommendations.'

He was watching her but not by a blink of an eyelash did she betray how she felt about the change of subject.

'Everything's as good,' she assured him, then she, too, pushed her plate aside. 'Even their desserts if you're a dessert man. And their coffee is something special, though I won't be indulging in it. I can hear my books calling me, and it will be a mug of instant in the study for me tonight.'

She pushed back her chair and he knew she was about to leave, but a slight hesitation gave him a chance and her own words suggested an opening.

'Hear the books calling from here? Where *do* you live?'

Her grin lit the golden lights again.

'Just down the road,' she told him, nodding towards the door where the street dropped down towards the railway line. 'Wrong side of the tracks to someone in the towers on the other side!'

She did leave then, threading a path through the tables, mostly empty this late at night, her slim body bending lithely as she made her way to the cash register.

Which is when he realised she was paying the bill.

Hers, or both?

He followed her, reaching her side as the woman she'd called Carole tallied the total.

'I'll get this,' he said, but Sally was having none of it.

'No fraternisation, remember,' she said to him. 'We each pay our own. He's my boss,' she added to Carole.

'Lucky you,' the young woman said, casting Grant a mischievous smile. She fiddled once more with buttons on the cash register, then said, 'But if he's your boss, he must earn more. Why not let him pay?'

Let's see you get out of that, Grant thought, but his resident was more than ready for an argument.

'And let him think I owe him something?' Sally retorted, handing Carole a note and waiting for change. 'No way. Anyway, it's his rule we're following. No fraternisation among the staff. Quaint, isn't it?'

He knew she was teasing but he bit anyway.

'You've just finished telling me you approve of it,' he reminded her, taking the slip of paper that he assumed was his bill from a fascinated Carole.

'Only because it happens to suit me at the moment,' Sally replied, turning towards him so he could see her impish smile. 'But who knows? You bring a tall, dark and handsome newcomer onto the team and my views on the subject might change.'

'You want someone more tall, dark and handsome than this man?' Carole demanded. 'You must need your eyes tested.'

And although Grant knew he should be offended, being discussed in the third person as if he weren't there, he nonetheless waited anxiously for Sally to reply.

'He's spoken for,' she said, swinging back to take her change and, as she dropped a few gold-coloured coins in a small glass bowl that must hold tips, she gave a theatrical sigh. 'Isn't that always the way?'

On that tantalising note, she started towards the door, then swung back.

'Thanks for your company at dinner,' she said. 'See you tomorrow.'

And with that she was gone.

'She's looking a lot better,' Carole said, and although Grant, not wanting to gossip about a staff member, didn't ask the obvious, the phrase puzzled him.

Better than what? He remembered her talking about taking time off. Had she been ill?

Or had the relationship she'd mentioned really hurt her? So deeply she didn't want to get involved with anyone again?

He sighed as he added his tip to the glass bowl. Then he thanked Carole and departed, heading for his car on the nearly deserted street.

He could understand Sally's wariness if a relationship had caused her pain. Hadn't he steered clear of all women for a long time after Erica?

But the thought of Sally in pain disturbed him and he looked up and down the road, searching for her. Perhaps she'd driven off.

Then, as he turned on his headlights, he saw the movement and realised she was walking down the road.

More uneasiness grabbed at his guts.

Was that wise?

OK, the street was quiet, and quite well lit except at the point she'd reached when he turned on his lights. At the corner, a big old mango tree leant over the fence and threw black shadows on the footpath. But as he put the car into gear and let it roll down the hill, the beam of light lit up her figure for an instant, then she disappeared beneath the tree.

He saw the gate as he drove past. Sally Cochrane lived in the old high-set house behind the mango tree. He'd noticed the place before and had admired the wide verandahs, but, like so many of the old wooden Queenslanders in this area, it was in need of a lot of attention.

He drove under the railway line and up towards the next hill and his apartment block, thinking it might be fun to do up one of those old houses. Bring it back to its former glory.

Sally Cochrane doesn't want you in her life and she definitely doesn't need any distractions this year, he reminded himself.

But, for some reason, he could see himself in an old shirt and paint-stained shorts, stroking green paint around the railing of Sally Cochrane's verandah.

'Now there's a puzzle for Dr Freud,' he muttered as he pushed his keycard into the box to open the garage doors. 'Green paint? Verandah railings?'

'Sounds like a nesting syndrome to me,' his infuriating brother said, when Grant called to him a little later and mentioned the possibility of buying an old house. 'I do hope it's the pretty resident.'

'Just because you've finally fallen in love doesn't mean I have to follow suit,' Grant told him. 'Pain we might share, but not emotions. Believe me, mate, love clouds too many of the real issues in a marriage. Like who takes the responsibility for what. Whose career comes first? Whether to have kids, and who's going to be their primary carer if you go that way?'

'Well, something must be working,' Tom reminded him. 'People have been muddling along, with love and marriage linked together, for a long time now.'

'Not always successfully,' Grant reminded him.

'And are all your operations one hundred per cent successful?' Tom demanded. 'Doesn't it depend on how success is measured?'

Grant glared at the phone.

'This is a ridiculous conversation. All I said was that I was thinking of buying an old house. Because I don't think I'd like to live in an apartment for ever, not because I want to get married.'

Tom's laughter irritated him even more, so he pleaded having another call on the line and hung up on his brother. Who was a damn fool. Fancying himself in love with a woman he barely knew!

He blocked the thought that he didn't know Sally Cochrane all that well either but, instead of going into his library to check something he'd need for a lecture the following day, he walked out on to his balcony and peered around the buttress that separated it from the balcony next door.

His apartment looked north and east, towards the city and the river, but if he leaned out a little further, he could see the railway line, and beyond that…

'Falling to your death while trying to identify a house behind a mango tree would be a stupid way to die,' he told himself, and walked back inside.

Tomorrow he'd phone Jocelyn, apologise again for all the missed dinners and arrange something for the weekend. It *was* time to think of marriage, but he knew it would work better with a pragmatic approach. He didn't need the love thing. Been there and done that! Seen the ravages it caused in other people's lives.

A sensible arrangement, that's what he required.

Which was another reason to get Sally Cochrane right out of his mind.

It took a mammoth effort of will but eventually Sally was able to immerse herself in the chapter she'd set aside for that night's work. She'd scheduled to finish this book by the end of the week, and start on the next over the weekend. Not that her schedules always worked the way she hoped. The singer from her brothers' band was visiting relatives down south and she'd be filling in for her this Saturday night, so the more she got done during the week, the further ahead she'd be by the time she had to leave the books.

Motor neuron disorders. Daniel's specialty. He'd offered to work with her, lend her notes, help her study. In the flat he'd rented, presumably so he had somewhere to stay closer to the hospital than his home in the outer suburbs. Somewhere, she realised now, where he could take the women with whom he cheated on his wife.

And to think she'd thought, back when he'd made the offer, he was being helpful! Had fallen for it. Once!

She forced her attention back to the books, back to the lists of disorders that could produce damage to the nerve pathways and leave a patient disabled.

Her eyes drifted from the pages. Towards the window. Above the screen of mango leaves she could see the top of the building where Grant Hudson lived.

'But not his apartment. It's on the other side,' she reminded herself aloud. 'And gazing at a glass and concrete tower won't get you through your exams. Put him out of your mind.'

Easier said than done, she admitted next morning when they dead-heated in the car park and so had to share a lift up to the ward.

'What are you? A workaholic?' he demanded, tapping his watch to remind her it wasn't yet seven o'clock.

'When I'm going to be in theatre, I like to see the patients before they're given their pre-op medication,' she said. 'And if you weren't here yourself you wouldn't know what time I started. Talk about the pot calling the kettle black!'

He chuckled and for some reason the day seem brighter—more exciting—although it had barely begun!

'Do you know Mr Fielding? Has he been a patient here before?'

The questions diverted her back to thoughts of work, rather than bright days, and she told herself she was pleased as they directed the conversation back on track. This was work—nothing more or less.

'He had an acoustic neuroma removed two years ago, but recent scans show a mass on the site.'

Grant nodded.

'He's certainly showing symptoms of something happening there,' he said, ushering Sally out of the lift. 'Vertigo, and tinnitus. Head pain. I know its hard to remove all of a neuroma because of its proximity to the brain stem, but it's unusual for there to be such a quick regrowth of a benign tumour.'

'Aren't we operating on him today?' Sally asked. 'Hadn't you decided that's what it was?'

Grant nodded, but he looked sufficiently worried for Sally to take it further.

'Second thoughts?'

He smiled at her, and her heart forgot she wasn't interested in him, *and* about the no-fraternisation rule, and began to tap-dance on her ribs.

'Second, third, fourth and fifth thoughts. I think I'll re-schedule him for later in the day and get Daniel to organise more scans this morning.'

'Radiology *will* be pleased,' Sally told him. 'Nothing they love more than rush pre-op jobs.'

'Better for them to be put out than to operate on a man I'm not convinced needs a repeat of major surgery.'

His tone told Sally the subject was closed. They'd halted outside the ward.

'So, will we shift the other surgical patients one place forward?'

'Who's on the list? Do you know? Will the second patient be here yet? Prepped? Surely not.' He answered his own question and Sally realised he was thinking out loud and stayed silent.

'The neuroma was scheduled for four hours minimum,' he continued. 'Damn. I should have reorganised this yesterday, but it was only as I drove to work I began to wonder if it might not be fluid clouding the image. There could be some scar tissue as well, but I'm not convinced it's a regrowth.'

'Couldn't we keep him as first patient but just drill an exploratory burr hole? Wouldn't that tell you more than a scan? And if there's fluid present, you could drain it off. Consider a shunt.'

His smile was slow coming, but when it did arrive it warmed bits of Sally she hadn't realised were cold.

'Smart kid, aren't you?'

'Not such a kid,' she retorted, then regretted the words as his eyes agreed with them.

'No!' he said, and pushed through the doors into the ward.

They separated, Grant to speak to the charge nurse, while Sally checked on the patients who were being settled into their rooms before the pre-op procedures began.

'You cutting today, Sally?'

Bill Dixon, the anaesthetist, was ahead of her, and Sally flinched at the description of her job.

'Operating sounds far less violent,' she told him. 'And before you begin on Mr Fielding, you might check with the boss. He's thinking exploratory rather than craniotomy.'

'Suits me,' Bill told her, and he drifted off towards the nurses' station where Grant was still discussing patients.

Sally also left Mr Fielding for later. Best for Grant to explain what he intended doing. She moved on to Mrs Nash, a stroke patient. Some weeks earlier, they'd operated to relieve pressure from fluid build-up, and had inserted a shunt, but fluctuating temperature and tests of the CSF showed an infection present, possibly from the shunt.

'How are you feeling?' she asked the woman.

Mrs Nash lifted her left hand and waggled it to signify so-so. Until the set-back with the fluid build-up, her speech had been improving.

'It's been a nuisance, hasn't it?' Sally told her. 'Never mind. Hopefully we'll have you right after this op. It isn't a big one. Dr Hudson feels if we remove the shunt the infection might settle down. There are other ways we can drain the fluid so don't worry about that.'

The patient nodded and reached out to take Sally's hand. Her thank you was rough, but Sally smiled and nodded to show she'd understood.

'No worries!' she said. 'It's all part of the service.'

But as she moved away from the woman, she was frowning. Mrs Nash was thirty. Mother of a young family. Too young to be so incapacitated.

Later in the day, as she worked on this particular patient, with Grant Hudson beside her at the table, the thought came back to her.

'Is it my imagination, or are we getting more and more young stroke victims?' she asked, directing the question not specifically at him but at the room in general.

'I've been wondering that,' Bill replied. 'Though, mind you, years ago, surgery wasn't considered part of a stroke victim's treatment, so maybe that's why we're noticing them more.'

'It's still not standard treatment,' Grant reminded them.

'Unless there's a bleeder to be tied off or, as in this case, a buildup of fluid following the insult.'

'Insult!' Andy said. 'I do love the use of that word. A blood vessel blows apart in someone's brain and we call it an insult!'

Sally chuckled, pleased to find the atmosphere in Grant's operations was improving.

'It might be a subject you could pursue, Sally.' Her boss came in on cue, as if her thinking about him had prodded him to speech. 'Pull together some figures on it. Present something to the students.'

'Right, when I've finished splitting a couple of atoms and building a new pyramid,' she retorted, her voice muffled as she bent over the eyepieces of the microscope and carefully inserted a probe towards the shunt.

She touched the spring release on the probe and tiny claws opened, allowing her to grasp the shunt and carefully draw it out.

'We'll flush with antibiotics,' Grant told Andy, 'as soon as Sally has it clear.'

'Good work,' he added, and Sally felt her skin heat at the praise.

But it was too good to last—this easing of the tension in the operating theatre, the unspoken truce between herself and the boss. Though why he'd suddenly gone cold again, Sally had no idea.

Perhaps he hated being called in for emergencies, she told herself late on Saturday night as she stood peering into the microscope while he probed bits of a shattered skull from the soft brain tissue of a road accident victim. Well, she hadn't particularly enjoyed coming straight from the night-club gig herself, especially as it had meant leaving the boys in the lurch.

She was handling the light source. Not easy when the

waves of coldness emanating from Grant's body made her shiver in the usually overheated theatre.

It had started in the changing room.

Could he be back on that mixed changing room campaign again?

Part of her mind darted through possibilities while she concentrated on what was happening in the work section.

Grant eased another piece of bone from the soft tissue and dropped it into a dish.

'Damn fools speeding up and down the highways,' he growled. 'With the road authorities showing graphic pictures of accidents on television, you'd think people would get the message about the damage speed can do!'

'Maybe we've got to bring speedsters into the operating theatre, or make them spend time in rehab units, to get the message across,' Harry Strutt, who was duty anaesthetist, suggested.

One of the nurses responded, but Grant dropped out of the conversation. He'd used speed victims to vent a little spleen, but the real cause of his unreasonable anger was standing right beside him, pressed hip to hip, as they shared the microscope.

He'd finally perfected a means of entering the changing room without his eyes going immediately to Sally Cochrane's usual space, and had even developed a technique for blotting out the sight of her when she came in later.

But tonight nothing had worked.

In fact, the arrival of his resident in a minuscule, glittery gold dress and some kind of gold dust highlighting her hair had temporarily stopped his breath and sent rampant messages of desire coursing through his body.

In fact, rampant was an apt description of his problem.

His first instinct had been to move closer. See if the excuse for a dress she was wearing was really as revealing as that first glimpse had suggested. His second, when a young intern had come in and whistled loudly to show his appreciation, had been to cover her with a sheet.

Things had gone from bad to worse when she'd casually stripped off the scrap of gold and revealed not the usual neat white cotton undies but fluffy bits of lace and satin in the same colour as the almost-dress!

'I understood you were far too busy studying to have a social life!' The terse comment grated from his lips as he made his way out of the room.

She spun to face him, revealing lusciously swelling breasts above the lace and satin.

'I understood it was none of your business,' she retorted, then she pulled her theatre top over her head and scattered gold glitter everywhere.

'Shower that out before you come to Theatre,' he told her, flicking a tiny golden star from his chest. 'What our patients don't need is gold dust in their brains.'

She glared at him and stomped off to the showers, and that was the last he saw of her until she appeared, fully gowned and scrubbed, in Theatre.

But if images of a weary but determined Sally Cochrane, bent over her books in the study of the house behind the mango tree, had been bothersome, this new image of Sally Cochrane, dressed to play, was beyond classification.

He forced himself to concentrate on extracting pieces of the depressed fracture. He shouldn't have offered to take Daniel's calls this weekend, though the idea of Daniel seeing Sally in—and out of—the gold dress only made him feel worse.

'That's it! Flush it well then we'll see if we can patch the depressed section back in.'

'The chips of bone have done a lot of damage,' Sally remarked, as she used a saline and antibiotic solution to flood the area.

'Speed kills!' Grant reminded her. 'He's lucky not to be

dead. You close him up. I'll check on what's happening next door.'

He walked away, knowing the initial count in the accident had been four badly head-injured victims. They'd operated on this lad first, as his injuries, apart from cuts and contusions, had been confined to his head. In the theatre next to theirs, thoracic surgeons were battling to seal a torn aorta, and it would only be if they succeeded that the neuro team would have a second patient.

The other two, once broken limbs were pieced back together, would be observed overnight. Closely observed. Cracked skulls often healed themselves, but at the first sign of increased pressure or a change in the patient's status, emergency surgery would be needed.

He stripped off his mask, gown and gloves, washed his hands, then walked down the corridor.

'Still working on him,' Abe Coulter told him when Grant poked his head into Theatre Five.

Grant nodded and backed out. Time for a cup of coffee. He'd make a pot, as the rest of the team would hit the tearoom before too long.

He was fossicking in the cupboard for a new packet of biscuits when Sally and the intern arrived.

'No patient yet?' she asked, as if totally unaware of any tension between them.

'They're still trying to stop the bleeding in his chest.'

'Why do they get the first go?' Paul Adams asked. He was young and keen but his enthusiasm for work, especially at two in the morning, made Grant feel tired.

'Not much use our saving his brain if they can't get blood to it,' Sally told the intern. 'We use brain death as a marker of exactly when a person dies, but without the oxygen carried by the blood the brain can't function.'

'So—'

Whatever Paul had been about to say was interrupted by

the arrival of a large, hearty male. He bounded into the room, and gave Sally a hug, then nodded genially to the other two men.

'Uh-oh, the vultures are gathering,' Sally said, extricating herself from the man's arms with a slowness Grant found infuriating. 'When did you get back?'

She addressed the giant, who flashed a smile her way.

'Miss me, did you?'

'No,' Sally told him, 'but I think Dr Hudson's new since you departed for foreign parts. David Phillips, meet Grant Hudson.'

'New neuro boss?' the man called David said, extending an oversized paw towards Grant. 'Lucky you, having Sally on your team. I tried to talk her onto my team but would she listen? Silly woman has some idea that waiting around for someone to die casts a shadow over transplants.'

'Who's going to die?' Grant asked, surprised to find himself in total agreement with his resident.

On this issue, at least.

'Chap with the blown aorta, I'd say. Wouldn't you?'

David had helped himself to coffee by now, and put his hand, unerringly, on the fresh packet of biscuits.

'Not necessarily,' Grant told him. 'In fact, Abe seems to think they've plugged the leak.'

That wasn't quite true, but Grant suddenly felt a proprietorial interest in the patient in Theatre Five. He wanted him to live.

And recover.

'We can help so many people these days.' David settled into an armchair as he spoke and Grant knew he'd sensed the atmosphere in the room and was trying to ease things over. 'I mean, one liver can ease the suffering of maybe three children. Corneas restore sight. Tonight we have a myocardopathy patient, a young woman barely thirty, standing by—'

'But if the aorta's torn, can you use the heart?' Sally asked him. 'A torn aorta is usually a seat-belt injury. Wouldn't the force of a collision that does such damage also cause tears or ruptures in the heart?'

'Not in this heart, dear heart,' David assured her, reaching out and patting her on the arm. 'Scan shows it's in A1 condition.'

Grant saw Sally shudder at the seemingly callous conversation, but she hadn't pulled her hand away from the man's touch.

Was there something going on between them?

She claimed she had no time for a relationship, but if the man had been away...

'How's Cherry?'

Sally's question startled Grant out of his muddled thoughts, and the smile on David's face told him the rest. The man was a toucher. One of those people to whom physical contact was important. As he described what must be his wife's advancing pregnancy, his face aglow with pride and excitement, Grant felt a sense of loss.

Maybe it *was* time to think seriously of marriage and a family.

Though leaving Jocelyn to get a cab home after dinner, earlier this evening, hadn't advanced his project of establishing a sensible partnership!

CHAPTER SEVEN

AND his body's reaction on seeing a gold-wrapped rear end poking out from under the bonnet of a car a little later threw another set of doubts into the concept.

'Trouble?' Grant asked, coming to stand beside Sally and peer ineffectually at the mechanical bits surrounding the engine of her car.

'Bloody clunker!' she growled. 'I swear this is the last time. I'm going to get myself a decent car if I have to sell my soul to do it.'

She turned as if uncertain who'd joined her in the early dawn light of the car park.

'And to make matters worse, the one time I really needed them, I didn't have a change of clothes in my locker, so I'm not only prancing around the hospital in cloth of gold but I've got oil on the damn dress.'

She stood up and indicated a dark streak running across her flat stomach.

'It'd be different if they paid me,' she muttered, but before Grant could question this bizarre statement, issued in conjunction with the sexy dress, she slammed down the bonnet and strode determinedly towards the street.

He hurried to catch up.

'Where are you going?'

She turned and looked at him, frowning slightly as if only now realising who he was.

'To hail a cab. I'm getting out of this place. The car can stay there. With any luck Security might tow it away and I can report it stolen and claim the insurance.'

She spun away and continued on her chosen path, a direct route to the main road beyond the hospital walls.

Once again it took Grant a moment to get moving so once again he had to lope after her.

'I'll drive you home,' he said, grabbing her by the arm so she couldn't escape again. 'I'm going that way.'

This time the look she gave him was more wary than puzzled.

'I don't bite,' he said, and suddenly she smiled.

'I'm sorry. I was rattled. First of all losing that lad—right there on the table after the thoracic boys had done such a good job of patching his aorta. Then not having any decent clothes to put on. I probably flooded the engine because I was anxious to get away.'

He heard a weariness that was close to defeat leaking into her voice, and was startled—and deeply affected—by it. Everything he knew of Sally Cochrane told him she was a fighter. Though losing a patient they'd fought so hard to save affected everyone, himself included.

'Come on,' he said gently. 'I'll take you home.'

Taking her by the arm, he led her to his car, unlocking it with the remote, then opening the passenger door and settling her into the soft leather seat, leaning across her slim body to fasten the seat belt.

He smelt the hint of flowers, that so light and elusive fragrance she wore, and saw the streak of black oil on the gleaming gold. Touched it with his fingers.

'Will it wash out?' he asked.

She lifted her head and their eyes met. Her lips were so close it was all he could do to not drop a kiss on them.

Then she smiled, and warning signs flashed in his head.

'I guess so,' she admitted. 'And the car will start tomorrow, *and* we'll save the next young man who tries to kill himself in a speed machine.'

'That's better,' he told her, then he did drop a kiss, very lightly, on her lips.

'What did you go and do that for?' Sally demanded, when she'd regained enough breath for speech, her palpitations had settled slightly, and Grant had taken his seat beside her.

'It was comfort, nothing more,' he told her, fiddling the key towards the lock and staring straight out through the windscreen. 'You were upset. Your lips were there.'

'You can't go around kissing lips just because they're there,' she told him. 'You'll get into all kinds of trouble.'

He didn't reply, merely starting the engine, with a gentle purr not a cough and splutter, then selecting 'drive', releasing the brake and steering the car smoothly towards the road.

All of which annoyed Sally even more. Particularly as his profile, which was all she could see of his face, revealed no trace of emotion. It might as well have been carved in stone.

'And you don't believe in fraternisation among your team,' she reminded him. 'What's a kiss if it's not fraternisation?'

Ha! That got him. He shot a fulminating glare her way and swung right onto the dawn-deserted street.

'It was comfort, that's what, and I'm damned if I know why I did it. But I sure as hell regret it since you're now being a typical woman and making a federal case out of it.'

'I'm being a typical woman?' Sally demanded, sure her voice had gone shrill with outrage. 'Well, in case you hadn't noticed, I *am* a woman, and pretty typical at that, so don't use it as a put-down, Grant Hudson. Just because you don't like women very much!'

The car lurched to a halt at the side of the road, and the driver, his hands clenched whitely on the steering-wheel, turned to face her.

Uh-oh!

'Where did that remark come from?' he demanded, scowling so fiercely his eyes seemed to shoot blue sparks. 'What makes you think I don't like women? You barely know me,

Sally Cochrane, so what makes you such an expert on my likes and dislikes?'

Sally straightened in the seat. So she might have gone too far, but there was no way this man going to browbeat her.

'This fraternisation thing!' she pointed out. 'What's that but an excuse to not get involved?'

'That really bothers you, doesn't it?' Grant said, dangerously quiet now. 'Why? Would you like to fraternise, Sally?'

He leaned closer, and Sally knew the heat sweeping through her body would show itself in her skin any moment.

'Not with you,' she muttered, denying the physical messages and relying on an instinct which told her it was dangerous to play with fire.

'With Daniel perhaps?'

The question was so surprising it startled her out of a moment of weakness when fraternisation had seemed like a good idea.

She squirmed back against the window, to get her body a little further away from the force field of Grant's.

'Most definitely not! He's married, and I happen to believe that women should stick together. Carrying on with another woman's husband is not my idea of female solidarity.'

The words struck Grant with such force he sat back in his seat and wondered what on earth he'd been doing to let this woman get to him. He'd stopped the car, intending to either strangle her or kiss her, and suddenly they were discussing marital ethics.

'I must be mad!' he muttered, rubbing his hands over his face in an effort to restore his senses.

Then he turned towards his passenger as he restarted the engine.

'How come you always manage to rile me in some way?'

She frowned as if she didn't understand the question, then she shrugged, physically pushing it away.

Physically moving those swelling breasts above the shiny gold dress.

And finally, as he swung the car back into the traffic lane, she answered him, a cheeky smile on her lips and the gold lights dancing again in her eyes as she said, 'Perhaps because you don't like women very much?'

Grant shook his head, held his breath for a minute so he wouldn't explode, then said, very calmly for a man battling a multitude of emotions, 'If I wasn't too tired to think through the consequences, I would stop this car again and show you just how much I don't like women.'

Which shut Sally up for the rest of the short drive home.

'Thank you for the lift,' she murmured when he pulled up beneath the overhanging branches of the mango tree. Then she was out of the car, and through the gate, whisking away as if a thousand devils were on her tail.

He sat there in the quiet stillness of the early morning, peering through the paling fence, hearing her light footfalls on the steps, across the verandah, a key fitting into a lock, then a door opening.

And closing.

What on earth had made him say the things he had? His head pounded with regrets and tiredness as he drove under the railway line and up towards his home. Was it because she'd taunted him with words, or because he couldn't handle his reaction to the sight of her in the sexy gold dress?

It was Tom's fault. All his talk of love and marriage must be having a twin effect on his, Grant's, psyche.

And libido!

Sally tiptoed through the house, seeking refuge in the bathroom where she stripped off her clothes and stood under the shower until it ran cold. The water would heat again before the boys were out of bed, and right now she needed the comfort, the warmth, of water streaming over her.

But although she usually found it easier to think under the shower—in water, by water, or underwater, for that matter—today the water failed to work its magic and she eventually turned it off, and emerged shrivelled, but no less confused.

Was Grant Hudson so attracted to her that he'd kissed her?

Probably not, if the way he'd yelled at her later was any guide.

Did she want him attracted to her?

Definitely not at the moment. She was having enough trouble concentrating on her books without the distraction of a love affair to make matters worse.

Did she want a love affair with Grant Hudson?

This question made her shiver so she wrapped her towelling robe tightly around her body and padded out of the steamy room.

Sleep on it, her mother had always said.

But would sleep come when her hormones were all a-twitter and her body ached for something it had never truly known?

She woke refreshed but no wiser five hours later, and decided to tackle the books. Again clad in the familiar comfort of her old towelling robe, and armed with a pot of coffee and a sandwich, she made her way to the study.

But reading about aneurysms reminded her of Grant Hudson's special skill, and images of his face, his blue eyes darting fury, came between her and the words.

When movement in the house told her the boys were stirring, she gave up. She'd get a lift to the hospital, and check on the survivors of last night's accident. Had the two they hadn't operated on stabilised?

She wandered back to her bedroom to pull on jeans and a silky knit shirt that was casual enough to feel like a day off but respectable enough to visit patients. As she was going to the hospital anyway, she might as well do a quick round.

Brad, the brother nearest to her in age, was in the kitchen, filling the kettle.

'I didn't realise you were home,' he told her. 'Where's your car?'

'In the hospital car park. It went on strike. I'm sorry about having to leave so suddenly last night.'

He leant towards her and gave her a brotherly peck on the cheek.

'No problem. We understand that when you've got to go you've got to go, but if you could fill in again next week, Meggie swears she'll be back the week after.'

Sally smiled at him.

'She'd better be! I should be able to do it, although it will mean juggling duty hours. And in exchange for the favour, would you drive me over to collect my car when you've had your coffee?'

She picked up the paper Brad had dropped on the table, but a photo of the shattered remnants of two smashed cars made her set it quickly aside.

'Your emergency?' Brad asked, pushing a mug of coffee across the table to her.

'We lost one of them. Operated on one—he's touch and go—and we're watching the other two.'

'Stupid fools,' her brother said. As a policeman he probably saw worse sights than she did, but at least it helped him understand how she was feeling.

'How did you get home?'

Sally sipped the coffee, giving herself time for the spasm of reaction in her body to ease. It was typical of Brad, who had appointed himself in charge of her welfare, to ask this question.

'The boss gave me a lift.' She nodded to where the tall building sat on the hill across the railway line. 'He lives over there.'

'Getting on OK with him?'

Sally nodded again. As far as she was concerned, 'OK' covered a lot of ground.

'How's the study?'

She put down her coffee mug and looked up at her brother who was slouched against the kitchen bench.

'Why the questions?'

He grinned at her.

'Brotherly love?'

'I don't think so,' Sally told him.

Brad hesitated, then rubbed his unshaven chin, and turned to look out the window to where another mango tree grew in the back yard.

Sally knew he'd be looking at the old swing, and the tangle of ropes she and her three brothers had used to get up into their secret world among the branches.

'We got to talking last night. Eddie, Phil and I. In the breaks after you left.'

He swung back and faced her.

'Seems to us you got the fuzzy end of the lollipop right from the start. When Dad died you were the one who helped Mum through. You not only followed Dad's dream for you to be a doctor, but you insisted we all get a proper education and bullied us into studying. You worked your own way through university, and got scholarships to pay for books, and all the time you were still there for Mum.'

Sally felt her eyes mist, but she rallied, although she had to swallow hard to do it.

'Hey! You all helped,' she reminded him. 'We stuck to-gether. We're a family, that's what we do. Although if some of you came unstuck soon, I wouldn't care. Shopping for the lot of you is like shopping for the army.'

'I knew you'd say that, about us all helping, the family stuff, but you did the most. Then last year, instead of taking your exams, you stopped work to nurse Mum. And even now, Meggie's away so you immediately rearrange your life to help us out in the band. When did you ever do anything for Sally? For yourself? What about *your* life?'

He paused, then added, 'Haven't you put it on hold long enough, Sister Sal?'

No one had called her that for so long—it had been her father's pet name for her— she had to blink and swallow again.

'My life's just fine,' she told her brother. 'Once I'm through these exams, and properly qualified, the world will be my oyster.'

But Brad couldn't have been convinced, for he leant forward and took her hand.

'But is that all you want of life? Work? A career? To be the best darned neurosurgeon in the world? What about fun, Sally? And love? Marriage and kids?'

She stared at her brother. Why had he brought up these things today of all days? Could he read her new vulnerability? Her confusion over whether a career *was* the be-all and end-all of life? Of her life?

Finding she couldn't handle the subject sitting down, she stood up and walked to the window.

'Funny questions for a Sunday morning, Brad,' she said lightly, and was surprised to see a shadow cross his face.

Then he smiled.

'Not when I was talking to Meggie most of last night,' he admitted, a shy smile hovering around his lips. 'Well, it was more like all the early hours of the morning, really.'

He took Sally's hand and held it as he explained. 'I hadn't realised until she went away how much I miss her. We're going to get married. As soon as she gets back, we'll start to organise things.'

He grinned at his sister, 'So one of us will be coming unstuck.'

'And Phil's been thinking of moving in with Francie,' Sally remembered, picking up on his last remark first. 'The three of you were talking about me because you're worried I'll fall to pieces if you all suddenly leave home. Poor old spinster Sally, pining away beneath the mangoes.'

Brad chuckled, and put his arms around her.

'Forget about Phil! You're supposed to be congratulating me,' he said, and she did, telling him how happy she was for both of them. She gave him a hug, and assured him of her delight.

Her very genuine delight, for Meggie was a lovely young woman and Sally wanted nothing more than for her brothers to be happy.

So why should she feel glum?

'Come on, finish your coffee and do whatever girl things you need to do then I'll drop you at the hospital.' Brad eased out of her embrace and patted her on the bottom to hurry her along. 'I want to call in and see Meggie's mother. Tell her what we've decided.'

Sally took her coffee and went, but her heart was full of so many conflicting emotions she wasn't sure how to handle them. She was still trying to sort through them as she made her way across the car park into the hospital a little later. Which might explain why she didn't see the figure step out from behind a van in the dimly lit underground section.

'And what, might I ask, are you doing here?' the figure queried as he deftly untangled her from his body and settled her on her feet. 'Shouldn't you still be sleeping?'

'Shouldn't you?' she retorted, pulling away from her boss's steadying hands. It *would* be him she'd trodden all over! Then, as he rubbed his calf where she'd undoubtedly clipped him with the toe of her shoe, she added, 'I'm sorry. I wasn't looking where I was going.'

'Lost in thought?' Grant asked.

She shook her head, then realised she had been, so she nodded. Which wasn't really an adequate explanation.

'My brother's getting married.' She forgot she was angry with Grant and the words, needing release, tumbled out.

'And that bothers you?' Grant asked, taking her arm and steering her towards the lift.

'Not really,' she admitted. 'In fact, I'm very happy for him and Meggie.'

'Sure! You sound quite overcome with joy!'

Sally frowned at him.

'Well, I am,' she snapped. 'It's all the other things I'm having problems with.'

'Would food help?' he asked. 'I came in to check on our patients, but as I still haven't shopped, I thought I'd grab a late breakfast or an early lunch in the cafeteria.'

The 'no' she should have said failed to find its way out of her throat and she ended up accompanying him to the cafeteria where, fearing the effects of too much caffeine, she bought an orange juice and a fresh-baked blueberry muffin.

'So tell me about this brother. You have more than one, don't you? Will his getting married leave you with problems keeping your house? Is that what's worrying you?'

She sipped her juice, and crumbled the muffin in her fingers. Scanned her inner uneasiness and felt worse.

'It's nothing to do with the house,' she managed to say, but the lump that had been there earlier was growing in her throat again, and when Grant reached out and took her hand, capturing the restless fingers and dusting the crumbs off them, she felt the prickle of tears and knew she should leave.

Right now!

Before she made a fool of herself.

But the need to talk to someone was stronger and she lifted her head and looked at this man who was still a stranger.

'It's Mum! Her not being there to see her eldest son married. To miss their happiness, and the boys' successes. They're all growing up and will move away, and where it always used to be me worrying about them, now they're worried about me. Worried I'll moulder away, a lonely old spinster under the mango trees.'

Grant held her fingers tighter. He couldn't make sense of much of what Sally had said, but he'd sensed a real despair in her earlier when she'd run into him, and had guessed she'd needed to get things off her chest.

So, despite his good intentions to steer clear of her as much as possible, at least until he'd got over whatever it was he'd caught from Tom, here he was, holding her hand over the laminated table in the hospital cafeteria.

Which, given his antipathy to hospital gossip, was the one place he shouldn't be holding anyone's hand!

'What-ho? Something happening here I don't know about?'

The cheery greeting made him turn, and he felt the slim fingers he'd been holding snatched from his grasp.

David Phillips, the transplant surgeon, dropped his tray on the table and slumped into the chair beside Grant.

'We're just out of Theatre,' he added. 'I did the heart, but they've used other organs as well. It's hell to lose a patient on the table, as you guys did, but my young woman has a little girl and she'll be able to push her on a swing in a month or so.'

Grant saw Sally smile wanly at the man, and realised she was beyond carrying her share of the conversation. So, much as he wished the man had chosen any table but this, it was up to him to smooth things over.

'Good job,' he said. 'Are you eating while she's in Recovery? Staying on to see her when she goes to ICU?'

David nodded.

'Don't know about you, but I can't bear to leave things at the recovery stage. I like to see a patient tucked up in bed even if it is in the nude with pipes and tubes and leads all over them.'

Grant nodded.

'The "job's not done till it's done" syndrome,' he agreed.

Perhaps it was the agreement when he'd expected argument that caught David's attention, for he turned to Grant, and with a faint inclination of his head towards Sally raised an eyebrow.

'I saw that,' she snapped. 'There's nothing wrong with me and, no, you didn't interrupt anything.'

She looked at Grant.

'I'm going up to the ICU,' she said, 'then home. It's my day off and I've study to do.'

She matched action to the words, marching out of the room with a determined stride.

'Phew! What's bothering Sally?' David remarked.

'Her brother's getting married.'

Grant wasn't sure why he'd said this, but as it was the only firm information he'd got from his resident he passed it on. Maybe David could throw some light on why she was so upset.

'Brad? That's great. I'd have thought Sally would be pleased. She's been nagging him to do the right thing by that young woman of his for ages.'

'Something to do with her mother missing the wedding?' Grant recalled. 'Is her mother away?'

David raised his shaggy head.

'Ah!' he said, as if light now shone on the entire situation.

'Well, you might explain to me,' Grant told him, and the other man smiled.

'Sally's mother died last year. Found she had a fast growing cancer, too bad for treatment. Sally should have sat her finals but took time off to stay at home and care for her. I guess she's thinking of how her mother would have loved to see Brad married. There must be a lot of times when her grief threatens to overcome her, but she's a stubborn little thing—always has been—so she won't give in to it.'

He shouldn't have let her go, Grant thought as he assimilated this information. He should have taken her into his arms and held her close until the storm of emotion had passed.

The thought shocked him and he had to remind himself he didn't want to get involved with a colleague.

Particularly not with Sally Cochrane, who had the ability to muddle his usually ordered thoughts and tie his own emotions into knots. It had to be Tom's influence. Like when he, Grant, had had his appendix out and Tom had had to be sedated because his pain had been so intense.

Sally went first to the ICU, knowing Grant would probably be heading that way as soon as soon as he'd demolished his very substantial breakfast.

Which had undoubtedly grown cold while he'd let her rattle on about her brothers' concerns.

But if she checked on the young man with the depressed skull fracture—Nick, she thought his name was—then did a quick visit to the ward, she should be far enough ahead of Grant to avoid further conversation.

Given the embarrassment she was likely to feel, this was an excellent idea.

And would have worked if Craig Greenway hadn't greeted her with the news that he could now move his toes. He was demonstrating this miraculous feat when Grant arrived.

'So, Dr Cochrane, are you pleased we operated on him now?'

Craig looked from her to Grant, then back to her again.

'I argued for a scan first,' she admitted to the patient. 'But Dr Hudson was right. Time was the important factor.'

'You mean if you hadn't ripped that huge hole in my back when you did, I'd have been paralysed for life?' the patient asked her.

Sally nodded.

'Scanning first might have meant a slightly smaller hole,

out every minute the clot was there, it was doing more damage.' She nodded towards her boss. 'Good thing you had an
expert handy.'

Craig reached out, something he couldn't have done last
week, and touched her hand.

'But you did it for me. I won't forget that.'

Sally stayed a little longer, then excused herself, leaving
Craig to demonstrate his limited movement to Grant.

She was about to leave the ward when one of the nurses
called her back to check a medication order on a patient file.
She took the file and walked through to the office, wanting
to look up the drug prescribed before OK'ing it.

'Do you need a lift home or is the clunker running?'

Grant appeared at the door as she was shutting the fat
volume. He was smiling, perhaps to lessen the insult to her
car, and it was only her determination not to give in to her
internal reactions to the man that stopped her smiling back.

'The clunker, as you call it, is generally a most reliable
car,' she told him, frosting the words so he wouldn't think
she was exchanging pleasantries.

'The clunker, as *you* called it,' he reminded her, 'let you
down when you badly needed it.'

She watched the way his lips moved, remembered how
they'd felt—

No! It was dangerous to even think about that moment!

'Oh, go away!' Sally told him, although she knew she
shouldn't speak to her department head that way. But he
shouldn't have kissed her either. 'After the way you behaved
this morning, I'd rather walk home than accept a lift from
you.'

'I'll remember that,' he said, his lips still smiling slightly,
though his eyes were...

Wary?

Watchful?

Sally opened the drug book again so she didn't have to

look at him. He obviously had no idea of the effect he was having on her hormones, and she had to keep it that way. Apart from the futility of falling for a man who didn't want a relationship with a colleague, she had no time for dalliance right now.

No way was she throwing six years of medical studies and another four, actually close to five, years of specialty work down the drain to satisfy her sexual urges.

There's no way you want to get involved with her, Grant told himself as he obeyed her grouchy order and departed. Firstly, she's a colleague, and you know the problems that can cause. Secondly, she has exams looming and shouldn't be distracted, and thirdly.

He couldn't find a thirdly, remembering instead how soft her lips had felt, how sweet they'd tasted.

How she'd looked in the gold dress…

He shook his head to clear it and went down to his office. A few hours of paperwork should prove sufficient distraction. And he'd leave a memo for Miss Flintock to make another appointment with the mighty Flo.

The mixed-sex changing rooms had to go!

CHAPTER EIGHT

THE week started as frantically as weeks usually did. Non-urgent cases were lined up over the weekend to be treated on Monday, so Mondays were always extraordinarily busy.

This particular week, Tuesday and Wednesday were just as bad, so Sally had little time to be brooding over kisses, and her body was tired enough for the physical effect of Grant Hudson to be minimised.

Handleable!

By Thursday she was able to leave early, taking time off to make up for extra hours she'd worked over the weekend. She was even able to concentrate on study and congratulated herself for getting back on track.

So the tap on the study door startled her and when Eddie, at twenty-one the youngest of her brothers, poked his head around the jamb, she let fly.

'Damn it, Eddie, you nearly gave me heart failure. I was so deep in the books I didn't hear you coming. Couldn't you have walked more loudly, or coughed?'

Eddie grinned at her, but it was another voice that said, 'I'll remember that next time.'

'Someone to see you, Sally,' Eddie added, when she'd already realised that and couldn't say she wasn't at home.

Grant's head appeared behind Eddie's and this time his lips weren't smiling, and his eyes were cold and hard.

'I need to speak to you,' he said, his voice making it quite clear—in case she'd missed the message in his eyes—that it wasn't a social call.

With a supreme effort of will, Sally didn't raise her hands to flatten down her hair although she knew her habit of run-

ning her fingers through it as she read would have left it
standing up every which way.

She did, however, tighten the belt of her ratty old bathrobe,
and regret not studying in something more...conventional?

'I suppose, as you're already here, I can't say no.' She
waved Eddie away as she made the grudging reply. 'If you
shift the pile of books off that chair you can sit down.'

A short afternoon sleep must have alleviated the numbing
effects of tiredness, for her body was in full response mode
again, nerves twittering away inside her, organs behaving
badly.

She watched the man lift the books then look around for
somewhere to put them.

'Use the floor,' she suggested, then let herself enjoy the
sight of his long body bending, with extraordinary grace for
a tall man, to set the pile on the floor.

But when he finally sat, and faced her, she forgot enjoyment. Grant Hudson was angry. Radiating tension so palpable
she could feel the waves zinging against her already sensi-
tised skin.

'I believe the mixed-sex changing rooms were your idea,'
he began, spitting the words out through clenched teeth.

Uh-oh!

Unable to think of anything to say—after all, the man was
right—Sally remained silent.

'Well, haven't you anything to say for yourself?' he demanded.

She held out her hands.

'What do you want me to say? Yes, it was my idea. That
it?'

The look he gave her should have shrivelled her skin.

'You know I've been against it. Right from when I first
arrived. You were even good enough to tell me I should see
Flo about it, but somehow you didn't see fit to explain it was

your campaign among the surgical staff that resulted in this ridiculous trial.'

He stood up, as if his anger was too hard to handle sitting down, but if he hoped to pace, he was out of luck. The piles of books all over the floor created too many obstacles for really forceful pacing.

He loomed over her instead.

'Well?' he demanded again.

'Well, what?' she retorted, getting tired of his browbeating attitude. 'You're making accusations, Dr Hudson, not asking questions. Do you want me to justify the idea? I'm sure if Flo's told you how we came to the decision, she's already given you my arguments.'

'I shouldn't have had to hear them from Flo!' he stormed, tripping over a prescription guide as the urge to pace over-came the obvious pitfalls. 'You should have had the decency to tell me.'

Sally rolled her chair back a little as the trip had landed him upright, but much closer to her desk.

'So you could yell at me like you're doing now?'

'I am not yelling,' he said, gritted teeth distorting the words.

'Of course you're yelling,' she told him. 'Yells can be just as menacing when they're quiet as when they're loud.'

She saw his reaction in the way he turned away from her, groaning his frustration, rubbing his hands through his hair, doing a little limited pacing before finally slumping back into the chair.

'Let's start again,' he said, after a pause long enough for him to have counted to ten at least ten times. 'According to Flo, because you're the one who promoted the mixed-changing rooms idea, you could also call off the trial before the three months is up.'

Sally, who'd felt a slight pang of sympathy for his frustration—having often felt it herself—forgot sympathy and rallied to the cause.

'Why would I want to do that?' she demanded.

'Because they're not working,' her boss declared.

'Who said?'

He blinked at her, as if he didn't understand the question, then hesitated, and she guessed he was discarding his original reply—'Me'—in favour of something more persuasive.

'I suppose it was some wonderful feminist idea,' he muttered. 'Equal rights in bars, women astronauts, then storming the last bastions of male exclusivity, hospital changing rooms.'

'It had nothing to do with feminism!' she told him. 'As if anyone cares about that in a hospital where females have been the prime force since time began. And the trial had the support of all the surgeons, male and female.'

His disbelieving look told her what he thought of that statement, though he didn't openly question it.

'Then how about you tell me why you wanted it?' he suggested.

She'd argued her case for so long, and so often, it should have been easy, but Grant's presence in her home, in the study she considered her own private sanctum, was unsettling her.

'It makes sense to me to change with other surgeons. That way, discussions of new techniques, talk of what's happening in surgery, is passed around.'

'It's passed around at medical specialists' meetings,' he reminded her. 'Far more often and far more effectively than it is in a changing room.'

Hmm.

She went to point two.

'Surgeons who'll be working together can discuss the operation ahead of them. Last-minute details, suggestions.'

'Do we do that?'

'If you mean you and me "we", then, no, we don't,' Sally said, anger building as he continued to snipe at her. 'But that might have something to do with the fact that you always change in the far corner of the room, out of everyone's way. I discuss what's ahead with Jerry and Andy—'

She was about to add 'and Daniel' but that wasn't true as she avoided changing near Daniel, usually going into a shower cubicle if he was in the room.

'Not Daniel?'

Of course Grant had picked up on it. Did he know her habits? Could she lie?

'All the other surgeons,' she replied, hoping she sounded casual and carefree enough for him to miss the evasion.

'So you'd say the trial was working?'

Sally tried to gauge his mood. He'd certainly calmed down but she sensed he was ready to pounce on her first unwary statement. She considered the—to her—unnatural silence in the mixed changing rooms.

'Perhaps not as well as I'd expected,' she admitted. 'But it's early days. Everyone has to get used to it.'

'Everyone won't have a chance to get used to it, Dr Cochrane,' Grant said softly. 'I want it stopped. I want the normal routine restored. Now. This week.'

'Why?'

She looked at him as she asked the question, her brown eyes puzzled where before they'd been wary. Grant tried desperately to think of an irrefutable argument. He could hardly say that while seeing her partly clad body had a bad effect on him, seeing partly clad men changing near her was even worse torture.

After all, it was ridiculous to be lusting after Sally's body. And he certainly had no right to feel proprietorial about it.

'Because it's not working,' he stated flatly. 'You said so yourself. The surgeons change in almost total silence. The

men are constrained because women are present and, n
doubt, the women are feeling exactly the same way.'

'You have no idea what the women are thinking,' she re
minded him.

'And don't I know it!' he told her. 'But I'm reasonabl
certain only a woman could possibly have seen any bene
in the idea.'

'Of course that's the case.'

He was taken aback to find her agreeing with him, an
before he could recover ground she struck.

'That's because the majority of surgeons are men. The
already change with each other. They've always had the in
terchange of ideas, the discussion about the upcoming ope
ation, the talk afterwards of how an op could have been be
tered.'

She glanced at him, as if checking to see he was listenin;
then continued. 'There might be only one woman on eac
team and with the old system she gets none of that feedbac
She might discuss similar things with the nurses, but then
week later the male surgeon she's working with mentior
she's using an instrument they'd decided to discard in favo
of something else and she realises the changing-room tal
has passed her by again.'

She had a point but there was no way he could concede
without losing his primary objective.

'So now no one gets feedback because of the total s
lence?'

The golden gleams in her dark eyes flared briefly, and h
guessed she'd been about to ease the rein on her temper, the
she smiled instead—all sweetness and light. 'Not even onc
they get used to it?'

'I don't think they will get used to it,' he said bluntl
Gold flares and cute smiles weren't going to put *him* o
track. 'I'm sure most of the men feel as I do—'

'Which is?' she interrupted, her eyes guileless now, and therefore doubly dangerous.

'Embarrassed!' he said bluntly. 'It's not quite a sports locker room situation, the changing rooms. We're not in the habit of parading stark naked around the place, but from time to time we might walk out of the shower cubicle in the nude to get clean clothes from a locker. We can't do that with women present.'

He hesitated, then decided to get it all off his chest.

'And then there's the other angle. Where to look when you're talking to a female colleague who's half-clad. What's normal and what's considered inappropriate behaviour? We poor bloody men can't win in those situations.'

For a moment he thought he had her, thought she was about to smile—perhaps give in—but when she did speak he realised how far wide of the mark he'd been.

Which confirmed how little he knew about women in general and this one in particular.

'So what you're saying is that women surgeons should continue to miss out on info-sharing to save the males a smidgen of embarrassment.' The dark gaze swept across his face. 'You might have to do better than that to convince Flo to stop the trial.'

Infuriated all over again, Grant stood up, inadvertently kicking over another pile of books.

'I should have known better than to waste my time talking to you,' he stormed, bending automatically and stacking the books back in a pile again. 'You're the most stubborn, argumentative female it's ever been my misfortune to know!'

And whatever Sally had to say about that was lost when the brother who'd shown him in—Eddie, he thought—reappeared, and said, 'Is your visitor staying to dinner, Sally?'

Grant wasn't sure which of their denials came first, but both the 'no's were equally forceful.

Eddie was apparently unfazed by this, simply murmuring,

'Pity! It's Phil's turn to cook and he's made a Moroccan thing with chicken and olives and apricots. Smells good enough to eat.'

And with this weak joke, he wandered off, leaving Grant to find his own way out of the old house. A way that took him past the kitchen where the delicious smell issuing forth made him regret his decision.

He still hadn't shopped!

The mixed changing rooms remained but Sally realised Grant had made his own arrangements, altering operating rosters so she was rarely on the same operating team as he was. She wondered if he'd also managed to exclude the women from other specialties who used the room, or if she'd been the only target.

Not that it bothered her, she told herself. The less she saw of him the better, and the unavoidable morning rounds were a big enough dose of Dr Hudson each day.

Friday came around again. Jerry was on duty for the weekend ahead and Daniel on call. Apart from Saturday night, when she'd be singing again, she'd have an unbroken stretch of study time ahead of her.

And an unbroken stretch of Grant-free hours, the better to steel herself against his appeal.

Yet as she drove home, close to midnight on Saturday, she couldn't resist looking up at the tower. Her eyes counted up the levels while she waited for the traffic light to change to allow her to turn right off the wide riverfront drive and into the street that skirted the hill on which Grant's building stood and led under the railway lines to her home.

Strange that he should live so close.

She thought of the previous weekend, when he'd not only driven her home but had offered comfort the following morning.

Strange that he could prove so human.

Not strange—bad! Far better that he remain inhuman—the robot head of department not a flesh-and-blood man.

It had to be tiredness causing these idle fancies, she decided as the green arrow finally gave her permission to move. She swung the car off the well-lit drive and into the tree-lined side street. Heard the chug of protest, the gasping cough—and silence.

'Bloody car!'

She steered it to the kerb and slapped the steering wheel in frustration. Since the fuel gauge had given up the ghost three months ago, she'd made a point of filling the tank every week.

But this week...

She rested her head on her arms and thought for a moment. She had her mobile and should phone a cab.

Then have the cabbie curse because it was such a short trip?

Or call the auto club and get them to bring petrol?

And wait an hour for them to arrive?

The easiest thing was to walk the few blocks home and get one of the boys to sort out the car tomorrow. The area was a quiet residential one, not known for street kids, hoodlums or drug addicts. In fact, break-ins were so rare they had no insurance excesses.

And the walk would do her good.

If she went up the hill, and cut down the next side street...

She grabbed her handbag, opened the door, climbed out of the car, locked it, swung the keys into her fist, warm and solid feeling, and set out. So it was stupid to walk up the hill then back down again, but she gave in to the impulse, allowing her eyes, once again, to count their way up the floors of the tall building ahead and on her left. Was that Grant's apartment?

The one with the lights still on?

Was this pathetic or not?

She was mocking herself, pointing out it was behaviour more worthy of an adolescent than a mature woman, when the figures appeared from a dark patch of shadow.

Silent and menacing, they grabbed at her handbag, the force spinning her around.

Instinct made her grip it tightly, and she tried to scream but inhibitions she hadn't known she had turned the noise into a pathetic bleat.

But even that small cry must have spooked her assailants for their efforts accelerated and she felt a savage blow to her right shoulder, then she was dragged to the ground.

The spectre of rape cleared her mind. She'd wrestled with her brothers all her life. Let them have the bag, and use your feet.

The two instructions came from nowhere, but she obeyed them instantly, flinging her handbag towards the gutter so at least one would have to move towards it, then pulling her knees towards her chest and kicking upward as the second person came towards her.

He flew backward, confirming an instinctive knowledge that they were young and slight.

Built for speed?

Sally didn't wait to find out. She scrambled up and set off, legs pumping, heart heaving, heading towards the lighted car park of the apartment building.

Footsteps echoed behind her, growing closer, accelerating her panic, so when she reached the lights and dashed towards the wide glass doors that protected the apartment dwellers from intruders, she didn't stop to consider pressing any bell but the one she knew.

Grant Hudson's.

Heard his voice—startled but not sleepy! She registered that much and even felt some relief she hadn't woken him.

'It's Sally. Someone chased me, took my handbag.'

She heard his curse, then something buzzed, but the adrenalin rush was over and her knees gave out, so when he came thundering out through the front doors she was still crouched beneath the doorbells, her body shaking so much she couldn't make her legs work.

'I-I'm sorry,' she managed to stutter. 'I shouldn't have come here, but it was closest. I was scared. The car stopped and I thought I'd walk. Stupid, stupid, stupid thing to do.'

She could feel his hands running over her body, seeking injuries before moving her. It was a normal thing for a doctor to do, but it added to her tension and she shrank back against the wall.

'I'm all right. Not hurt. I need a cab and some money to pay it if you wouldn't mind.'

She looked at him, and saw both anger and confusion in his eyes.

Shouldn't have come here, Sally.

'I'm sorry!' she muttered, but he swept away the apology with a wave of his hand.

Grant squatted on the marble step and tried to make sense of what was happening. He'd felt a hot rush of anger when he'd heard Sally's faltering voice, then fear, colder and sharper than shards of ice, had killed it, and he'd come rushing down to find—

A woman with spiked hair and a sinful red dress so revealing it should have been censored.

Last week it had been shimmering gold and there'd been gold dust in her hair.

What did she do on Saturday nights?

For which she wasn't paid?

And why did the questions make him feel queasy?

He shook his head.

He'd think about them later. Right now, this woman needed help.

'Come on. Let's get you upstairs,' he said and gently eased her to her feet.

He would have liked to have carried her but after the scare she'd had, further helplessness might panic her.

She struggled to find her balance, kicking off one remaining red shoe, trying to stand alone, but needing his support to manage.

Then, to his surprise, she tried a wobbly smile.

'I'll be all right,' she assured him. 'I realise I lost it there for a few minutes, but I really will be OK. If I could just get cleaned up, perhaps beg a cup of coffee from you. They didn't hurt me, you know. I threw my bag and kicked the one who knocked me down, then I ran.'

Grant felt his anger surge again, but rushing down the road to belt a couple of punks was hardly sensible. Not when Sally needed help more than she needed revenge.

He used the key he'd grabbed as he'd left the apartment to get them into the lobby, then helped her across to the lift, and held her as they rose to his floor.

Jocelyn was standing in the open door of his apartment, presumably waiting for an explanation of his abrupt departure.

'What on earth—?' she began, but Grant, who'd have liked a couple of explanatory statements himself, stalled her.

'Put the kettle on, would you, Joss?' he said. 'And have a dig around in the little bar cupboard. See if Tom included brandy when he stocked up.'

He half led, half carried Sally to an armchair and lowered her carefully into it. In the clearer light of his living room, the red spikes of hair standing up all over her head were even more startling, while the shimmering red dress, what there was of it, looked so sexy it was indecent.

'I'll be right back,' he said, turning abruptly away from the mesmerising sight.

With a blanket, he told himself grimly. Covering her will help more than her shock!

He found a face washer and dampened it with warm water,

tucked a blanket under his arm, and returned, slightly more in control, to where his unexpected visitor was huddled in the chair.

He covered her first, then sat beside her, banking down new anger when he saw the grazes on her face.

With a gentleness usually reserved for very new babies, he bathed away the dirt, washed scrapes of blood from one bare shoulder, then, as she held out her hands to him, as trusting as a child, he carefully wiped away the grit and more blood.

'Thank you,' she whispered, and the huskiness in her voice warned him not to look into her eyes.

But he couldn't help himself, and when he saw the shimmer of tears, a growl escaped his throat, and he tucked the blanket more tightly around her, then held her close.

'You'll be OK,' he promised her. 'I'll look after you.'

'And how does she take her coffee? Do you know that?'

Jocelyn's voice was iced with contempt.

Grant ignored the icing.

'Make it sweet and milky. Did you find brandy?'

Small struggles and a muted sniffle from the bundle in his arms suggested she might be trying to get free, so he settled Sally back into the depths of the chair, handed her a handkerchief and went in search of the brandy himself.

'And just who is she?' Jocelyn demanded, her muted whisper echoing around the kitchen.

'One of my residents,' Grant told her bluntly, hoping she'd take the hint and not pursue the matter.

'Your resident? What happened to her? Not that I'd be surprised. Tarted up like that, a woman is asking for trouble.'

'Unfortunately, walking the streets at night, no matter what she looks like, a woman is asking for trouble.'

At the sound of the flatly delivered statement, Grant spun around to see Sally, unwrapped again, standing in the doorway.

She smiled apologetically at him and added, 'I didn't mean

to eavesdrop, but I needed the bathroom.' She paused, then lifted a hand to brush it across the spikes on her head and added, 'In fact, if you wouldn't mind, I'd like to take a shower. Running up the hill made me sweat and all the red must be dripping out of my hair. I'm worried it'll get all over your blanket.'

He closed his eyes for a moment, then opened them again. No. It wasn't a dream. Sally Cochrane, in red spiked hair and a dress that should have been illegal, was still standing there. A little stain on a blanket would have been a cheap price to pay for sanity!

'I'll show you where the bathroom is,' Jocelyn volunteered, although her voice suggested she'd sooner be showing the way to the front door.

'Here, take the coffee, and see she drinks it.' Grant shoved it into Jocelyn's hands. 'Stay in there with her in case she develops a delayed reaction of some kind. There are clean towels hanging on the rails and I'll pass in a towelling robe.'

He dismissed as unworthy a thought that if Jocelyn hadn't been here, it would have been his role to stand guard against an unexpected reaction.

Voyeurism, that's all it would be! he scolded himself as the two women disappeared, leaving him alone with uncomfortable thoughts.

'I showed her into the spare bedroom. Told her to rest for a while then I'll drive her home,' Jocelyn announced, striding back into the living room some time later. He'd been staring out at the view and trying to make sense of a number of disparate reactions, and not getting far. 'Apparently she lives close by.'

Grant heard the words and guessed Jocelyn was waiting for him to tell her she needn't go. In fact, he'd sensed earlier that she'd been angling for an invitation to stay.

Which probably explained why he'd still been awake,

ready to do a Sir Galahad act, when Sally had come ringing on his bell.

'Did she tell you any more about what happened?' he asked, avoiding the pitfalls of any other discussion.

'Only that her car had stopped and she'd decided to walk home. And something about her brothers being angry, and them playing in a band, but it didn't make much sense.'

Jocelyn pursed disapproving lips.

'Sex, drugs and rock and roll,' Grant murmured.

'What do you mean?'

He looked vaguely at the woman he'd known for so long—and with whom, at one time, he'd even contemplated a close relationship.

'I've no idea,' he said. 'It's just a phrase that keeps repeating itself in my head.' Then, realising he must sound demented, he smiled and added, 'Look. There's no need for you to stay. I'll let Sally have a rest then drop her home later. No sense both of us being up all night.'

'I don't have to go, Grant,' Jocelyn said, bringing his assumptions out into the open.

He leant forward and kissed her on the cheek.

'It's best you do,' he said gently. 'I'm not Tom for all I look like him. And if you think about it, and are really honest with yourself, what you and he had died a long time ago.'

He took her in his arms and held her close.

'Time to move on, Joss. I'll always be your friend. You know that. But the man you need is still out there somewhere. Waiting for you.'

He felt her slack body grow taut a split second before she pulled away from him.

'You won't even give it a chance!' she stormed. 'You're like Tom. You won't admit it but you're still seeking something special. There *is* no magic, Grant. It doesn't exist. There's friendship and sharing and tolerance and understanding. Common interests and companionship. That's what marriage is about.'

She stalked off towards the kitchen where she retrieved her handbag, but as she whirled towards the door she stopped and flicked her head towards the passage—towards the spare bedroom.

'And if you think that—that woman is going to bring you happiness, then think again!'

He heard the slam as the door swung back on its hinges and hit the wall, and pulled himself together, following Jocelyn out, joining her in the lift, speaking quietly to her, anxious to calm her down before she got behind the wheel of her car.

Agreeing with her helped. Acknowledging all the points she'd made as being the right ingredients for marriage. Talking, talking, talking—while his limbs grew heavy and his brain felt dead.

Promising to phone her in the morning finally did the trick.

Though he knew he'd regret it, because it would take them back to square one—to her assumption that something could develop between them.

But as he made his way back up to his apartment, concerned about his patient—he'd been gone at least an hour— he remembered something Jocelyn had said and smiled grimly to himself.

No, he didn't think 'that woman' was going to bring him happiness. A certain level of frustration—definitely. Odd spurts of anger when he felt baffled by something she said or did. A constant sense of being slightly off balance when he was with her.

Of being somehow at a loss when he wasn't.

All of these things she'd already managed to inject into his normally placid existence.

But happiness?

With Sally Cochrane?

CHAPTER NINE

SALLY was standing by the window in the living room when Grant returned. A robe-wrapped shadow in the faint glow shed from the light still burning in the kitchen. The red spikes were gone and familiar dark hair now clung damply to her shapely skull.

'Can I get you something?' he asked, wary about approaching her when she'd been assaulted by members of his sex.

She shook her head.

'No, thanks. I was thinking I should phone someone. The police. My bank. Report the credit cards missing.'

The tremor in her voice gave her away and he went to her and once again, knowing no other way to offer comfort, held her close against his body.

She was shaking. More shock than cold, he suspected, although he didn't tell her that when she said apologetically, 'I can't seem to get warm.'

'Just relax,' he told her. 'Come. Sit with me. I'll make the phone calls.'

He led her to the couch and tucked her against his side, keeping her anchored there with one hand so his body could feed warmth into hers. One-handed, he flicked through the phone book, found the necessary numbers and made the calls.

'The police want you to call at the local station tomorrow to sign a complaint,' he eventually reported to her. 'Your credit cards are cancelled. What about your car? Should I call the auto club to shift it for you? Were the keys in your handbag?'

. She opened her hand and looked down at it, as if expecting them to be there.

'They were in my hand. I'm sure I didn't drop them. I remember thinking that if I hit out with them it might hurt more.'

He thought of how she'd huddled into the chair and glanced across there. The keys were squashed into the soft leather, against the armrest.

'Apparently you did hang onto them.' He pointed to them and was pleased to see her smile.

'Well, that saves a call to hospital security, doesn't it?' she said, and moved away from him, fumbling to hold closed the opening of the robe. 'I should be going. You've done more than enough on my account. Did your friend go home? I'm sorry. I've spoiled your evening.'

'My friend was leaving anyway,' Grant said, surprising himself by the firmness in his tone.

The conversation stalled.

Think practical, he told himself, but his wayward mind was trekking down paths so far from practical it was downright embarrassing.

'Will there be someone at your place? These brothers of yours? Will they keep an eye on you? You could easily have a delayed reaction.'

'The b-boys!' she stuttered, and the brown eyes gazed into his with such helplessness that if he'd been able to get his hands on the louts who'd hurt her, he'd probably have murdered them. 'I can't tell them. They'd be angry at me for walking alone. At whoever did it. They'd go crazy about the whole thing.'

She tried a wobbly smile and added, 'They're a bit protective.'

'And so they should be,' Grant growled, knowing exactly what she meant as he'd felt the same reactions himself. He pulled himself together and suggested the obvious. 'Stay here

for the night. I'll run you home in the morning before their
stomach alarms have them up and about. Then you can tell
them in your own time.'

Sally looked at him with puzzled eyes and he touched her
cheek with the tip of his forefinger.

'You'll have to tell them some time, you know.'

The brown eyes, gold flecks subdued, studied him and he
realised that, although she nodded her agreement, she hadn't
lost the puzzled look.

And why he thought kissing her would help, he had no
idea, but he did it anyway. Leaning forward and kissing her
very softly on the lips. Catching her soft gasp of surprise in
his mouth, tasting the remains of sugared coffee, then only
the woman.

At first, she let him have his way, remaining quiescent but
not cold. But when he slid his tongue between her lips, she
responded, not tentative so much as taking her own sweet
time to explore his lips, his mouth, as he'd explored hers.

Her body pressed closer, and when the edges of the robe
opened enough to expose a swelling breast, common sense
sounded a warning in his head.

'This is a bad move,' he managed to say, though his hand
hadn't listened to common sense and was testing the weight
of that breast, his thumb rubbing, ever so gently, over a hard-
ening nipple.

'It's adrenalin,' she murmured in reply, coming closer instead of moving further away. 'I know that, Grant, but it
doesn't seem to make any difference.'

Her own hand had been engaged in exploratory manoeu-
vres and he knew just how aware she was of his arousal.

'We're consenting adults, after all, and we both know it
doesn't mean anything.'

He felt the words like Braille against his lips and knew he
should stop kissing her, stop relishing the silky smooth skin
beneath his fingers.

Be sensible.

But she was doing sensible, and for some reason he was finding the murmur of her voice, the calmly stated assertions of it not meaning anything—about it being nothing more than mutual comfort—unbearably erotic.

He gave himself up to kissing, then somehow they were lying on the couch, not sitting, though when he felt her fingers slide under his shirt, the discomfort of the situation—not to mention the stupidity of going further—struck him as forcibly as a blow from a bit of four by two.

He straightened up, and put her from him, looking into her eyes so he wouldn't see pert breasts, slightly flushed from his fingers, and will-sapping silky skin.

'Not a good idea, Dr Cochrane,' he said firmly.

Little smile wrinkles appeared beside her eyes.

'I know that,' she told him, 'but it *would* be nice.' The gold glints seemed to sparkle as she added, 'Don't you think?'

He groaned and buried his head in his hands. The golden glints were as bad for his anatomy as the damn breasts.

'Of course I think it would be nice, but is that all you want? Nice?'

She reached out and took his hands, easing them away from his face so he had to look at her again. He could read a measure of his own uncertainty in her eyes, but there was something else as well. A flicker of excitement, as if she'd listened to the sage advice her head had, no doubt, offered her and then discarded it.

'Sometimes nice is more than enough,' she said quietly. 'Tonight, nice sounds like heaven to me. I know it's reaction, Grant, but it feels right. To lie together, enjoy each other. Give and take some pleasure. No strings, no promises, no regrets tomorrow.'

She paused, the flicker growing into something stronger, steadier, then added, 'Would it be so bad?'

Yes, his head was shouting, but his body had stopped listening. He leant forward and once again kissed her gently on the lips.

'That sounds like talk, Dr Cochrane,' he said. 'Especially the bit about no regrets tomorrow! Why are you so sure you can handle that?'

She kissed him back, then pulled away, pressing little teasing, smoochy kisses on his neck before replying.

'Why is it men believe the love-'em-and-leave-'em scenario is a purely male preserve?' she asked, her eyes dancing with the knowledge that she'd shocked him. 'I'm not promiscuous, Dr Hudson. Far from it, but when it comes to mutual pleasure and satisfaction, aren't women just as entitled to it as men?'

Grant shook his head, unable to believe, firstly, that he was having this conversation with his prim resident and, secondly, that he was continuing to find it almost unbearably arousing.

'You're saying a romp in the hay, so to speak—a one-night stand—is all you want? All other women want?'

She grinned at him.

'I must admit I'm every bit as surprised about this as you are,' she said in her usual forthright manner, 'and while I don't have a clue about how other women think about it, right now, tonight, I am very sure that what I want is a one-night stand, as you so indelicately put it, with you.'

And if anything was going to put him off, Sally decided, stating it so bluntly should. She had no idea why she was talking this way, or why spending the night, or what was left of it, in bed with Grant Hudson should suddenly be so important.

Sally knew he wanted her. She was sitting too close to know his ardour hadn't dimmed.

Perhaps if she explained how she was feeling.

Or tried to.

She edged closer and began.

'For a long time now, I've had other people I've had to put first,' she said, holding his hand and rubbing her thumb across the palm as she carefully selected each word. 'Other people, or study, or responsibility of some kind.'

She looked up into his eyes.

'Tonight would be just for me. Just for pleasure.'

She gave a little choke of laughter and added, 'Great timing, huh?'

The silence went on for so long she was afraid swallowing might break it, and in the end, deciding he was trying to figure out how to say no without hurting her feelings, she cracked.

'But, of course, you've your own considerations. Jocelyn, or some other lover you wouldn't want to betray. I understand that. Stupid suggestion.'

She pulled the robe closed across her chest and shifted further along the lounge, wanting to be sure her legs would hold her up before she made an as-dignified-as-possible exit.

Grant snagged her with one foot, and somehow tumbled her back into his arms.

'Just for tonight?' he growled, biting playfully at her neck.

She managed to nod, words beyond her now it seemed vaguely possible.

'Mutual pleasure?'

His thumb rasped against her nipple.

Sally nodded again, then her lips opened to his demands and she relaxed, letting her body show him what it wanted, responding to his as a dancer responded to almost forgotten but once familiar music.

Sally woke slowly, bits of her body coming to life in a random sequence. Her shoulder hurt. Her mind felt woozy but somehow contented. Her toes were tingly, but her neck ached, and there was a more pleasant ache deep inside her. Her back was warm where it nestled against a firm body.

Her back was warm where it *what*?

The question fairly shrieked through her mind and she froze, too afraid to move in case she woke the firm body.

Details of the previous evening's conversation came back with alarming clarity.

Uh-oh!

How could she have sat there on her boss's lounge and calmly asked him to please take her to bed?

What must he have thought when she'd virtually insisted?

What could he have done but oblige?

She bit her lip to stop the loud wail of regret that welled up inside her.

Not that she hadn't enjoyed it, but—

No regrets, she'd promised him, and she had none. Well, none if you discounted the fact that what they'd shared had made her feelings for him worse, not better.

But was she sorry it had happened?

She couldn't lie to herself about something so important.

No.

So no regrets!

Or complaints for that matter, the part of her that was reliving the experience suggested slyly. This man knew things Greg had never dreamt of.

But their professional life? All the tomorrows?

Could she meet him in the corridor and not think of how she'd cried out…?

Operate beside him and not remember how he'd made her feel?

And all this with a man who was against staff fraternisation?

She closed her eyes and wondered if it was possible to will oneself into oblivion. If she tried hard enough, could she transform herself into a puddle of ectoplasm and simply melt through the mattress?

You can pretend! she told herself firmly when will-power had failed to dematerialise her. Pretend it never happened.

And for starters, you can get out of his bed and go home. It's daylight, and as he's come from Sydney he's sure to own a lightweight overcoat. You can borrow it and scurry home and think about everything else some other time.

Like next century!

Totally spooked by her thoughts, Sally eased off the bed and slipped out of his bedroom. Remembered her need for cover and slipped back in to ransack his wardrobe.

No regrets! she'd promised him.

Hell, they hadn't even used protection. Had she really assured him it was quite safe? Given him the impression she was on the Pill?

After the way she'd talked about it being a woman's prerogative to indulge in one-night stands, he'd probably assumed it anyway!

Probably assumed a lot of things she'd prefer he didn't think about her.

She found a soft, camel-coloured coat and eased it off the hanger.

Mutual satisfaction, she'd said to him.

She hoped he'd had that.

But why had it happened? Why had her control broken last night of all nights?

Could fear have sent so much adrenalin pumping through her body that it hadn't only overcome her inhibitions about casual sex but had actually made her ache for that ultimate expression of close human contact?

'Let's hope you don't get attacked before a visit to the dentist,' she muttered grimly to herself, thinking of the overweight and, to her, unattractive dental surgeon who was always asking for a date. 'Or the accountant!'

He was tall and lean and bald, and treated her with an irritating benevolence!

But thinking about dentists and accountants was a mental ploy, she realised, to prevent her thinking about the real problem. Six feet something of super-sexy male who'd had her hormones in a frazzle even before she'd been stupid enough to leap into his bed.

Hell!

She pulled on damp underwear—pleased a determination to feel clean after the attack had prompted her to wash it last night—and the torn red dress. Wrapped the coat around her and tiptoed into the kitchen, seeking pen and paper.

Somehow, she had to make working with him again possible. And in order for her to face him without blushing a fiery red with mortification, she had to convince him the night had meant nothing to her.

That she'd meant what she'd said about it being nothing more than a release, a one-off interlude of mutual satisfaction.

But how?

'Borrowed your coat,' she wrote. 'Will bring it into work Monday.'

That was good. Practical and to the point, while making it obvious there'd be no post-mortem of the events later today.

She stopped and sucked on the end of the pen for a moment.

She should say thank you for his comfort—without detailing which bit had helped her most. But she couldn't figure how to word it, as everything she tried had connotations she didn't want to consider.

Thank you for taking me in?

No way!

In the end she settled for the two words.

'Thank you.'

Then she left the note where he'd see it, and quietly left the apartment.

'So she'll give the coat back Monday, will she?'

Grant ground the words out with a savagery that didn't begin to express his feelings.

Though why he'd been so furious to find Sally gone, he couldn't fathom.

Frustration was part of it. She'd been warm and responsive and alarmingly sexy, and his body had woken him with some extraordinary memories, and a strong desire to see if it had been as good as he remembered it.

So to find no warm body curled against his had been the first shock.

To find she'd disappeared completely had been the second. That's when muttered words about cheek and ingratitude had fuelled his anger.

Well, she could stay gone as far as he was concerned.

She'd been the one who'd insisted it was a one-night thing. No strings. No regrets.

And if that's what she wanted, that's what she'd get! Not by a flicker of an eyelid would he betray how he felt.

Which was how?

He groaned aloud when he realised he couldn't answer that question.

Confused, certainly. A little bit cheated.

Missing her?

Certainly not!

It had been purely sexual. He'd woken wanting more, and she'd been gone. Well, that was for the best. He'd go for a run instead. Get the paper. Enjoy a leisurely morning at home.

No complications.

Apart from an ache in his groin and a sense of loneliness he'd never felt before.

He reached for the phone. After all, Tom had to take some responsibility for this. It had to be his sudden and apparently overwhelming attraction to Sam that had prodded lust to life in Grant's usually controllable body.

'Do you believe women can think the same way men do about sex?' he demanded.

If Tom was startled by the request, he didn't show it.

'In what way? Enjoyment? I think the feminist movement finally convinced women it was OK to enjoy it.'

'I mean casual sex. With no strings? No hang-ups? No expecting lifelong commitment after a one-off bit of pleasure?'

There was a silence, then Tom said, 'Who is she? Tell me it's not Jocelyn who's got your gonads tied in knots.'

Grant glared at the phone.

'Why couldn't it be a purely rhetorical question?'

Tom's laughter echoed through the earpiece.

'Is she still there? In the bathroom? How did you meet her? What's her name?'

'She's not still here,' Grant told him crossly, then realised he'd given himself away. No longer a rhetorical she. 'And it doesn't matter who she is—all I want to know is whether you think it's possible for a woman to understand the concept of a one-night stand. No strings, no regrets.'

More silence, then Tom asked, 'Are you still so afraid of commitment you make these rules before you even begin a physical relationship with someone? Before you give things a chance? Did Erica mess you about that much?'

Glaring at the phone no longer seemed enough. Grant felt like strangling it.

'I didn't make the rules, as you call them,' he stormed down the line. 'As a matter of fact, she did!'

He heard his brother's bark of laughter and slammed the phone back into its cradle.

Hoped he'd punctured the bastard's eardrum!

But why did it matter?

Why shouldn't a woman seek physical pleasure from sex without wanting more?

Wouldn't that be an ideal situation?

The answers that came to him were totally unsatisfactory. Theoretically he accepted women had as much right to physical enjoyment as men had and, therefore, yes, they should be free to indulge in whatever form of sexual pleasure turned them on.

Though why he should be hoping Sally Cochrane *wasn't* like that, he couldn't say.

Sally made it her business to stay out of her boss's way. She'd dropped off his coat at his office Monday morning, avoiding both him and Miss Flintock by going in very early and leaving it, wrapped in brown paper but clearly labelled with his name, outside the outer office door.

Avoiding him on the official ward rounds, or in other situations where their paths inevitably crossed, was impossible, but she'd learned enough of his routine to steer clear of the ward at times he was likely to pop in, and she lengthened her own days so she could make earlier and later visits to patients both there and in the ICU.

So bumping into him, almost literally, in the library late the following Saturday afternoon was totally unexpected.

And seeing him in casual clothes, tailored trousers and a soft knit shirt in a dark blue colour which did wondrous things for his eyes, wasn't what she needed.

'Well, well,' he said. 'If it isn't the elusive Dr Cochrane.' His smile, false though she suspected it might be, made her pulse race. 'Is it my deodorant?' he added, still smirking at her as she skittered backwards.

'Your deodorant?' She sniffed suspiciously. 'What do you mean? Is it new? Overpowering?'

The smile widened, lighting up the eyes she found so be

guiling—and sending her nerves into a quivering dither of delight.

'Certainly not overpowering,' he said, with dry emphasis on the final word. 'In fact, I've been wondering if it was falling down on the job. If my proximity was to be avoided at all costs, but even my friends wouldn't tell me?'

She forgot quivering dithers of delight and frowned at him.

'What on earth are you talking about?'

'An old ad campaign my parents talk about. Even his friends wouldn't tell him. I thought it might have been body odour keeping you away from me.'

'D-don't be ridiculous,' she stuttered, but she couldn't stop herself sniffing the air again and adding candidly, 'Actually, there's no trace of body odour, and whatever aftershave you wear has a very pleasant lemon-grass tang to it.'

'So?' he persisted.

'So what?' she asked, scanning his face for some clue to this probing.

'So why are you avoiding me?'

'I'm not avoiding you,' she told him. 'In case you don't remember we did a ward round together this morning.'

'And operated together a few days back,' he reminded her. 'But unless I specifically make a time to see you, or it's a rostered duty, you're a flash of skirt disappearing around a corner, or a hint of flowers in the air after you've whisked from a room before I reach it.'

'A hint of flowers?' Sally repeated. 'Getting a bit poetic for a man who doesn't encourage fraternising in his team.'

'There's a difference between fraternisation and the occasional pertinent discussion between colleagues, Dr Cochrane.'

The ironic tone skated along Sally's nerves, but there was no way she intended weakening in her resolve to keep out of his way. Just being in the same hospital was enough to prod memories of 'that night', while operating near him had become a kind of agony.

But little meetings, one-on-one discussions in the privacy of Grant's office, were most definitely to be avoided. They provided far too much opportunity for delicate subjects to be raised.

Plus the possibility that she'd forget herself and gaze with longing at his lips, remembering…

'Was there anything in particular you wished to discuss? Some patient problem? Is it Craig? I would have thought you'd be pleased with his progress.'

He made a strange noise—part growl, part tooth-grinding—and glared at her, and something in his expression reminded her of the other man she'd met—the carbon copy.

'How's your brother?' she asked. 'Has he had scans? Is there any lingering after-effect of his concussion?'

Another strangled sound suggested it wasn't the best question to have asked, so she turned away to close the book she'd intended reading, knowing she'd find concentration impossible with him in the room.

But with the book closed there was nothing to pretend to read. Nowhere to look, except at Grant.

'Shall we begin again?' he said, then he held up a hand. 'And before you ask "begin what?" in that innocent voice of yours, which, incidentally, doesn't fool me for one instant, I mean begin this conversation. I'll admit I introduced the note of levity to it, and that it was a mistake so now I'll go the direct route. Are you deliberately avoiding me?'

Much as she disliked lying, Sally decided it was the only option.

'No,' she said, and looked directly into his eyes as she said it in the hope she'd make it more believable.

'That's it? No?'

The man sounded stunned—which made two of them, really, as the conversation was certainly throwing her for a loop.

'What else do you want me to say?' she demanded. 'I mean, if I'm not avoiding you then there's no reasoning to tack anything onto the statement, is there?'

He made the groaning noise again and turned away, taking several steps before swinging back to say, 'And my brother's fine, thank you. Yes, he did have a scan and, no, so far there've been no nasty repercussions.'

Then, with a nod that told her nothing, he disappeared behind a stack of files.

Sally's first impulse was to flee, but that would give credence to his suspicions, so she sat down and reopened the book, leafing through until she found the reference she'd already read. The one that had started her in search of a second text.

'Are you interested in Parkinson's as a subject for further study?' The sudden question made her start, then she felt a warm hand rest steadyingly on her shoulder.

'I'm sorry if I startled you,' Grant added.

The warm hand remained where it was, as if he'd forgotten he'd left it there. But Sally couldn't forget its presence—or ignore the little shimmy of excitement so casual a touch had generated.

'It's OK,' she managed to say. 'I'd become absorbed in what I was reading and thought you'd gone.'

'Of course!' he told her, his tone more dry than ironic this time.

'You asked about Parkinson's. About study.' She shifted so his hand slid from its position, forcing him to retrieve it. 'Not really. I mean, I'm not contemplating further detailed study of it, but the use of surgery to alleviate the worst of its symptoms does interest me. You know Harry? Harry Strutt? The anaesthetist who works nights?'

She was aware she must sound demented. Firing words

and mini-sentences at him like scatters of lead from a shot-gun. But the man's return, just when she'd managed to shut him out of her mind, had seriously damaged her composure.

Perhaps permanently, if the way she felt right now was any indication.

'Harry who did the anaesthetic for Craig's operation?'

Pleased he'd been able to follow her babble, Sally nodded.

'His wife has Parkinson's and Harry's her primary carer. Over the years, when I've been on nights, we've got into the habit of discussing it—new trials of drugs, alternative treatments. Harry actually knows a lot more than I do but I can't help feeling that eventually surgery will offer more than drugs.'

'Spoken like a true surgeon,' Grant said, then he leant across and lifted the book she'd been reading. 'But this isn't new. It's the standard text. Written what, twenty years ago?'

'Yes, but I remember reading somewhere a list of toxins suspected of causing the reduction of dopamine in some people.'

'Resulting in the onset of Parkinsonian symptoms?'

He sounded interested, and Sally, pleased to be able to discuss her thoughts, even with a man she was trying to avoid, nodded.

'Manganese? Carbon monoxide? Cyanide? Methanol?' he recited. 'They're the ones I can recall offhand, and a number of prescription drugs come into it as well. Why the interest in the toxins?'

His smile invited a response and, reluctantly, she let her lips relax.

Returned his smile.

'It was something I noticed on the website you mentioned. Apparently, one of the suggestions for further research is to test people for reactions to the known dopamine-reducing toxins as an early-warning system.'

'Seems a bit extreme to me. Have you tried Hurst? For the list?'

Sally shrugged at the mention of the book she'd failed to find.

'It's gone walkabout,' she told him. 'I suppose one copy could be out on loan but as it's a reference there should be a spare here at all times.'

'I've a copy at home,' Grant said, the words slipping easily into the air between them. 'I'm heading that way now and you're welcome to come over and borrow it. Or, if you prefer, I can bring it into work on Monday.'

Now *he* was scattering words like lead shot. Regretting the offer?

No! He sounded more anxious than regretful.

Anxious for her to say yes or no?

She didn't puzzle over that question for long. After all, if she had the book, she could spend tomorrow looking up the possible side effects of the toxins listed and give some thought to producing a paper on the dangers of taking theoretical research too far.

And going back to his apartment might kill some of the ghosts currently haunting her dreams. It would prove, both to her and to him, that she'd meant all the things she'd said. That it had been nothing more than a night of mutual pleasure.

No regrets.

Like hell!

But that was for her to know, and him not to guess.

'I'll come now,' she said decisively. Published papers added kudos to one's name and weight to job applications. And she could wave it in the face of her examiners later in the year.

Think work, Sally, and keep thinking work!

She reshelved the book which had failed to supply the list she wanted, and followed Grant out of the subterranean room.

Having separate cars made the drive easier, though apprehension gnawed at Sally's nerves.

And standing in the lift, being whisked upward, was even more unsettling. The walls seemed to close in, while the air sparked with the awareness which, hopefully, only she could feel.

But as he opened the door memories came flooding back and she faltered so it took a firm hand in the small of her back to actually get her over the threshold.

Into a room where one high-heeled, scarlet shoe sat, like a piece of sculpture, or perhaps a trophy, dead centre on the bar between the living room and kitchen.

CHAPTER TEN

I'LL ignore it, Sally decided. Won't even acknowledge it's mine. After all, its mate is long gone.

'Cup of coffee?' Grant offered.

'No, thanks!'

Definitely not! Being alone with him was bad enough, but now the air in the apartment was doing dreadful things to her skin. As if she'd left tangible memories of his kisses in the room, and they were now gravitating back towards her.

'I'll just get the book and go home.'

Grant understood this was his cue to head for the second bedroom which he used as a study, find Hurst and return with it in his hand, but his feet wouldn't move without direction, and right now his brain was too busy coping with memories of another Sally Cochrane to be providing help for his feet.

Though she certainly didn't seem fazed by it all. Standing there, cool, calm and very, very collected. A slight sprite of a woman in her figure-hugging jeans and cotton T-shirt.

Yet he was remembering her in the red dress.

And out of the red dress.

'Did the dress recover? I recall it was slightly torn.'

She looked startled for a moment, then smiled.

'I've other dresses,' she said.

'Like that?' he muttered, unable to believe the Sally Cochrane he'd met that night had been anything other than an aberration.

Although there'd been the gold dress the week before!

Her smile widened, and a glitter of something he didn't recognise sparked in her eyes.

'Short and tight, you mean?' She didn't wait for his reply. 'Dozens!'

Which made him feel almost as bad as acknowledging that some women, possibly Sally amongst them, *could* treat mutually satisfying sex as nothing more than a pleasant interlude.

She must have read some reaction in his face, because her smile hardened.

'Double standards, Dr Hudson? It's OK for men to go out to pick up a woman for the night, but not for a woman to do the same thing?'

'Why on earth would I be thinking that?' he demanded. 'What you wear is your own business. As is who you "pick up", as you so aptly put it. It has nothing to do with me at all.'

'Exactly,' she said crisply. 'Now, if I could trouble you for the book, I'll be off. Saturday night! Time to slip into something extremely short and slinky and go a-hunting again.'

This time the messages got through to his feet, which moved him swiftly from the room. He'd give her the damned book and get her out of here.

No matter that locking her in his bathroom—or better still, his bedroom—might seem like a far better idea.

He found the heavy volume and carried it back through to the living room.

'And where's the "in" place in Brisbane?' The question startled him as much as it appeared to startle Sally, but he pushed valiantly on. 'I'm new in town, remember.'

It took Sally a moment to register what he'd asked. She'd been busy chastising herself for her smart-alec answer to the dress question.

Something about nightclubs. In places? Though she wasn't interested herself, she knew she'd heard people talking about the latest bars and clubs, but for the life of her she couldn't put a name to one.

'Where do you go?' he persisted.

'City Rowers!'

She blurted out the words, hoping she had it right. The boys sometimes went to the riverside club after one of their gigs. Sometimes joined in an impromptu jam session. But even when she'd been younger, she'd usually gone home. Far more interested in sleep than partying.

'And is that where you're going tonight?'

A-hunting? Had she really used that word?

'P-perhaps,' she stuttered, then, hearing the desperation in her voice, she tried again. 'Though now I have the book I might have a night at home.'

His disbelieving look eroded several layers of skin, but she found a smile and flashed it at him, said a polite 'Thank you' and headed for the door.

'Don't you want your shoe?' he asked, his voice husky and somehow seductive.

But there was no way she was going to give in to husky or seductive. She waved a hand airily towards it.

'Oh, is that mine? Did I leave it here?'

'I found it downstairs the next morning,' he said, deliberately reminding her of how that evening had begun.

Sally hid her shiver of remembered fear, and stayed determinedly in her newly adopted character.

'Pity you didn't find its mate, but as that's gone, one's no good to me. You might as well keep it. Actually, it adds a bit of colour to your room. Like a retro *objet d'art*!'

She continued on her way towards the door, praying she'd sounded casual enough.

Though it was more likely she'd sounded plain demented.

Still, demented was better than besotted, which was a more accurate description of her inner state.

Grant let her go. No way was he getting back into a lift

with her. He'd had a hard enough time keeping his hands off her on the way up. Why tempt fate?

City Rowers.

Not that he intended going there in search of her.

No way.

He'd had good, sensible, practical reasons for putting his suggestion of no fraternisation in place, and all those reasons still held.

More strongly than ever, in fact.

The mere thought of Sally in a slinky, sexy dress, out on the prowl for a man, was enough to give him heartburn. Get any more entangled with her and he'd end up with a coronary.

Sally didn't turn up at City Rowers that Saturday night, and the following Saturday, when Tom was up from Sydney and Grant persuaded him and his now fiancée, Sam Abbot, to join him at the nightclub, Sally was again notable by her absence.

All he'd achieved had been smoke-smelling clothes which he'd had to send to the cleaners and a couple of headaches from the din.

At work she was unfailingly polite, and formally distant, her demeanour constantly reminding him of his own edict about fraternisation.

Talk about a stupid thing to have suggested!

Tom's temporary presence in his apartment, and his decision to get married before he returned to work, was causing enough chaos to distract Grant in his off-duty hours, so it was only when he lay in bed at night he felt the ache of loneliness, and only when he saw Sam and Tom together that envy ate into his soul.

'Do you want to invite anyone to the wedding?' Tom asked, when the last-minute invitations were going out. 'Jocelyn will be there, of course. Mum insisted she be asked as her parents are coming up from Sydney both to see her and to attend.'

He paused, as if waiting for a reply, then, when Grant remained silent said, 'Perhaps the owner of the red shoe?'

Grant's eyes went unerringly to the breakfast bar but the shoe was no longer there. He'd packed it away before Tom had arrived, but his brother must have come across it while rummaging through cupboards in search of something else.

'I found the red shoe,' Grant told him, and told himself it wasn't quite a lie.

Tom shrugged.

'OK, then. Up to you! But you've been as edgy as hell since I arrived. I thought I must be putting a damper on your social life. Keeping some woman from frequenting the place.'

'Just because you've decided to get hitched doesn't mean we both have to behave like jackasses,' Grant told him. 'That's taking the twin thing too far.'

But Tom wasn't put off by his grumpiness. He immediately launched into a defence of his decision then slid effortlessly into praise of his delightful Sam, leaving his brother's love life, or lack of it, alone.

In the week preceding the big day, Grant's accommodation was stretched even further by the arrival of his parents. A family dinner at Sam's grandmother's house was an occasion to introduce everyone to each other, and Grant had his first taste of Sam's twin brothers' humour.

'Ignore them as much as possible,' Sam advised. 'They're so caught up in the fact that we'll have a double dose of twins in the family, they'll drive you nuts, given half a chance.'

But Grant found them fun, and talking to them, sharing in the excitement that was infecting the air, made the days go faster and the nights a little easier.

The wedding day finally arrived. Grant stood beside his

brother, and had to swallow a lump in his throat when he saw the bride arrive, stars in her eyes as she walked towards them.

But the love and tenderness in Tom's eyes shook him even more. Maybe this love thing had something going for it.

Maybe he'd caught it, the way they'd always caught their childhood ailments from each other.

He glanced towards Sam, and in his mind saw dark shiny hair instead of red-gold curls beneath the veil. Gold-shot brown eyes instead of green.

Could he be sick?

Feverish?

Maybe it *was* an ailment!

'We need the ring.'

The minister's voice brought him back to reality. Grant handed it over, playing out his allotted role, even if he did feel detached, perhaps excluded, from the special magic happening right there in front of him.

There had to be sixty people in the church but he knew Tom and Sam were unaware of them, elevated to some plane above mere mortals by their feelings for each other.

The ceremony over, Grant took the arm of Sam's best friend, Patty, and followed the couple to the registry to do the paperwork. As the door closed behind them he heard music start up, then a voice, an alto, pure and strong, rising and falling with the notes of what sounded like a couple of guitars and a keyboard.

Singing songs of love.

'Who's that?' he whispered to Patty, a young woman from Sam's home town whom he'd first met at the dinner earlier in the week. 'There wasn't any singing at the rehearsal.'

'It's some cousin of Sam's,' Patty whispered back. 'Hasn't she got a gorgeous voice?'

But it was more than the voice. It was the seductive power

f the words, reaching him clearly even through the closed door.

The words of love.

For some reason they made him think of his aggravating resident.

Of her ridiculous conditions of no strings and no regrets.

He shook his head to clear it.

Words of love affecting him? Wasn't he cured of love?

It's emotion, he told himself. A surfeit of it, given this wedding business.

Nothing to do with Sally Cochrane.

The signing done, Patty adjusted Sam's long veil, then Tom took his bride's hand and together they walked back into the church.

The singing stopped and the traditional organ music took over as Dr and Mrs Tom Hudson greeted their guests. Grant and Patty followed the newly-weds down the aisle, then, as they reached the door and family closed in to kiss and congratulate the couple, Grant turned back into the church, dark after the daylight outside, hoping to see the songstress.

She was coming out of the choir stalls, candles on the altar throwing shadows on her slim, shapely legs as she stepped carefully down the steep stairs.

A cousin of Sam's!

His heart told him who it was before he recognised the gold dress.

Then one of the band members swept her into his arms and hugged her, and jealousy pounded like a disease in Grant's blood.

Caution forgotten, he strode up the aisle.

'You didn't tell me you'd be here!' He all but yelled the accusation at her.

'I didn't know I would be. I'm on duty so it was in the lap of the gods. Brad's fiancée, Meggie, would have filled in if I hadn't been able to make it.'

She was so darned calm, standing there with candlelight making her look utterly beautiful, chatting away as if they were in the ward discussing patients.

'You've met Eddie. Have you met Brad and Phil?'

As she introduced them, he realised these men were her brothers. He shook hands with them as Sally continued chatting.

'Meggie's outside,' she continued. 'She actually sings better than me but Sam wanted the family connection.'

'Meggie's been away, which was why Sally was filling in for us as band vocalist on Saturday nights,' Brad said to him. Then he nodded, and added, 'And now I've met you, thank you for what you did for her that night. I've told her how stupid she was, but I'm grateful. We all are. And we should have caught up with you earlier to tell you.'

Not wanting to be reminded of 'that' night, Grant waved away the gruff expression of gratitude.

The three brothers packed up their paraphernalia, nodded to him and walked away, leaving Grant and Sally alone in the small church.

'Well?' he said, and she had the cheek to smile at him.

'Well what?' she asked.

'You know well what!' he muttered. 'Why did you let me think you went out picking up men? And why mention that noisy place, City Rowers? If you knew how much sleep I've wasted at that nightclub!'

Her startled gasp gave him some satisfaction.

'Why would you have gone there?' she demanded.

'Because you made me think that's where you went. You did it deliberately. Don't come over all innocent with me, Sally Cochrane.'

'You asked what was a popular place and it was all I could think of,' she told him, the candles highlighting the golden gleams in her eyes. 'I didn't say I went there.'

'Splitting straws!' he muttered, knowing this conversation wasn't going anywhere near the way he wanted it to.

And wondering if it were possible that his own deepening inner turmoil might simply be a reflection of Tom's emotions on this, his wedding day.

'Grant, you're needed for photos.'

It had to be Jocelyn who'd been sent to summon him, which added to his aggravated reaction.

'You'd better go,' Sally said before he could protest. She looked more relieved than annoyed by the interruption.

'I'll see you later?' he asked, then realised hesitancy wasn't the best of approaches with Sally and turned the question into a statement. 'I *will* see you later.'

Sally watched as he followed Jocelyn out of the church, then she leant against the altar and fingered a velvety rose petal that had fallen from one of the pale roses in the central arrangement.

She'd known that coming to the wedding, having, out of politeness, to socialise with Grant Hudson, would be difficult. But seeing the carbon-copy brother standing there at the altar, pledging his love for Sam, had almost broken Sally's heart.

She'd been so busy denying the attraction between them, writing off what she felt as lust, it hadn't occurred to her that the feelings she had for Grant could possibly be love.

Yet when, from her perch in the choir stalls, she'd seen him walk in with his brother, identical men in identical dinner suits, she'd unerringly recognised 'her' Dr Hudson. And had had to press her hand against her breast to still the racing of her heart.

If it wasn't love, then it was coming close, she'd realised, and she'd spilled her feelings into the songs she'd sung when the bridal party had left the church to sign their wedding certificates.

'Are you OK, Sally?'

Eddie was standing halfway down an aisle and the fact

that he wasn't carrying his guitar told her he'd already been outside and had returned to look for her.

She dropped the bruised petal back on the gleaming wooden surface.

'I'm fine,' she said, and hurried to join him.

Outside, the bridal party had already been whisked off to a park for photographs, and guests were making their way to cars to drive back to the big family house at Toowong for the reception.

Sally waved away an offer to travel with Brad and Meggie in her brother's more reliable car.

'I'll take the clunker,' she said, knowing she might need it to escape if the tension got too much.

What she'd really like to do is go home. Plead study, or tiredness, or perhaps a touch of typhoid, to avoid what was to come.

But Grant's words—'I *will* see you later'—suggested he'd track her down, wherever she hid, and whatever excuse she offered.

For Grant the ensuing hours went so slowly he was burning with frustration by the time the official part of the evening was done and he could finally seek out the dark-haired, gold-clad nymph who'd hovered like a flickering candle in his peripheral vision all evening.

But was she to be found?

Not a sign of her, although he searched through the rooms, and walked around the wide verandahs.

'I think I saw her out by the pool a little earlier,' Sam's brother Pete—or maybe it was Sean—told him when he sought the help of someone who knew the layout of the rambling old house.

There were lights around the pool, but the thick growth of palms and tree-ferns threw patches of shadow, so standing on the verandah, peering down there, didn't help.

In the end, he made his way down the back steps and,

avoiding a couple—surely Jocelyn was one of the pair—kissing in the rockery, he walked out to the pool.

The gleam of gold gave Sally away. She was leaning on the fence, gazing up at the night sky, her back to the house and his approach.

He moved towards her, then, remembering how put out she always was when he, in her opinion, crept up on her, he called her name and saw the moonlight shimmer on her hair as she turned to face him.

'Sally?' he said again, for no other words would come, and when she didn't answer—didn't help him in any way—he let instinct be his guide. He took her in his arms, drew her close, looked down into her bewildered eyes and kissed her.

He'd hoped the kiss would say the things he didn't understand well enough to put into words, but all it did was make matters worse. It numbed his brain and made his blood run hot, and tempted him into reading things into the way Sally kissed him back.

'Should we tell her brothers? Send them to the rescue before he steals her virtue?'

The voice broke into his benumbed brain but it took a second longer for the words to make sense.

He lifted his head but kept Sally clamped against him. No way she was going to escape until more had been said.

One way or another!

He turned to Sam's brothers, who were lounging up against the fence at the other end of the pool.

'Could you two cut the comedy routine or find someone else to bother?'

'We were sent to find you,' Sean, or Pete, said virtuously.

'Your parents are leaving.' The second twin expanded on the statement. 'Wanted to let you know the lovely Jocelyn was giving them a lift back to your place, and to say goodbye.'

'My parents are leaving?' Why was he having so much trouble with simple conversations? 'But they can't go yet. The bride and groom—'

'Are long gone,' the twins chorused.

'Oh!'

Grant felt small hands pushing at his chest and realised Sally was trying to escape his hold.

'You go!' she whispered urgently. 'You have to do the right thing by your parents.'

'But I want you to meet them—them to meet you,' he said. 'And we have to talk.'

She'd finally managed to detach herself and now, as he looked down into her face, he saw her smile and felt his heart stop beating for a moment.

'Not tonight,' she said gently. 'Not like this.'

She lifted her hands and tried to smooth down the hair he'd been ruffling, then touched lips that even in the moonlight he could see looked slightly swollen—well kissed.

But he had to talk to her.

'Stay here,' he ordered, and raced towards the house. He'd see his parents off, explain he wouldn't be long, then say what had to be said to Sally.

'She left as soon as you dashed off,' one of the twins told him when he hurried back to the pool only five minutes later. 'Said something about study, or being on call, or some other excuse women seem obliged to offer.'

'Know so much about women, do you?' Grant snarled at the unfortunate young man, then he walked back through the house and out the front door. Which is when he realised she couldn't have left. He'd been standing in the drive, saying farewell to his parents. She'd have had to have walked past him and she certainly hadn't done that.

But another search of the house failed to find her and, seething with frustration, he finally gave up.

What he should do was drive straight to the house behind the mango trees and demand she listen to what he had to say.

Only his parents were waiting for him, expecting a post-mortem of the wedding, wanting to chat about his new job and life in Brisbane.

And he wasn't entirely certain what it was he wanted to say to Sally Cochrane anyway.

Or how to put it into words.

Sally knew it had been cowardly to run away. And as for jumping the side fence and going down the lane to get out to the main street, that had been downright deceitful!

But Grant Hudson, and his kisses, had filled her with so many contradictory feelings she needed time to work things out. Time to decide what to do about this attraction that was obviously not as one-sided as she'd been telling herself it was.

But her mind wouldn't work. Wouldn't even focus on the books she knew she had to read.

In the end, she gave up, and went over to the hospital. She'd do a ward round then go to the library. Maybe a change of scene would help her concentration.

Grant, who'd spent Sunday showing his parents around the parts he knew of Brisbane, was tense and anxious by the time he arrived at the hospital early on Monday morning.

Darned woman, running off like that! He'd...

What?

Tell her off? Yell at her?

Well, that would be one way to relieve a little of the frustration he was feeling.

Kissing her might be another, a seditious voice whispered in his head, and he groaned aloud, wondering if he'd ever feel 'normal' again.

'Heavy night?' An orderly passing must have heard the sound and had turned sympathetically towards him.

'You don't know the half of it, mate,' Grant told him, then he strode along the corridor, telling himself he'd better put Sally Cochrane right out of his mind and concentrate on work.

He checked the computer, noted which A and E patients had been admitted to Neurology's care over the weekend. Nothing flagged as urgent. Next he checked on the status of the previous week's accident victims, bringing up a computerised version of their charts to ensure there were no signs of deterioration in their status.

With nothing urgent calling him immediately to the wards, he'd tackle bookwork first. He had a pile of reports to check and sign, then the agenda for the surgical specialists' meeting to consider, a paper he should have posted last week to complete, and a pile of memos from Miss Flintock so high they could have replaced the confetti at the wedding.

But Sally hovered at the edges of his mind, distracting him, making each task a little more difficult.

He turned to the day's list, then to the staff. Thanks to the avoidance tactics he'd put into place earlier, he was operating this morning with Jerry and Andy, while Sally, Daniel and an intern were on this afternoon for small procedures.

Now the mixed changing-room business was ruining his private life!

He was brooding over this when the phone rang.

'Flo here, Dr Hudson. I've already spoken to the ward but wanted to let you know the morning's schedule will be put back by a couple of hours.'

'Why?' he demanded, knowing a morning change meant that whoever was last in line would be lopped off the list and have to wait for another day.

'Because your theatre has been in use since two this morning. Dr Denton thinks he'll be finished within the hour but then the cleaning staff have to get in.'

Grant tapped his computer screen to life and scrolled back

through the messages. When a neuro case was brought into A and E it was automatically recorded on the computerised list which came through to him each morning.

'Dr Denton's operating? There's nothing in the morning notices about a neuro case in Theatre.'

Having a neuro case in Theatre explained why it was their operating schedule in jeopardy. Daniel would be using what the team considered 'their' theatre.

There was a pause and he guessed Flo was rummaging through her own paperwork. After all, she wasn't on duty twenty-four hours a day so she would also have to rely on someone else's information to keep her files in order.

'Here it is,' she finally said. 'Two patients. Climbers. Injured when a rope gave way. They were airlifted in and Dr Denton was on call. Apparently Dr Cochrane was at the hospital when the call for the helicopter went out so she waited and she's assisting. The first patient is in Recovery, or may be on the way to the ICU by now, the second should come out of Theatre soon.'

'Well, the airlift explains why they're not on the list,' he said to Flo, while his mind puzzled over what Sally had been doing at the hospital. 'They'd have been stabilised in the air and gone straight to Theatre.'

Which didn't solve his other problem of surgical delays.

'Is there no other theatre available?' he asked, although he knew the answer.

Heard it in her chuckle.

'But if you can go through your list and shift one person out, I can give you an hour's overtime for staff at the end of the afternoon shift, so you'll only be one patient behind.'

Grant thanked her and accepted the compromise. Drew the list closer and began to study it, thinking of the hours for each procedure, and who could reasonably wait for another day. Phoned the ward to alert them, then, as he heard Miss

Flintock come into the outer office, he called her in to ask her to contact the patient who'd be 'bumped'.

He checked the time. Although this morning's ward round wasn't a student round, with both Daniel and Sally in Theatre, he'd have to take it. But if he hurried...

It was ridiculous to want to check on what was happening in Theatre, especially when even poking his head in the door meant changing into pyjamas, slippers, cap and mask.

But at least he wouldn't have to scrub, he consoled himself as he hastily shed his clothes.

From the instructions Daniel was giving—no wonder he irritated the other surgeons—Sally must be closing. Grant stood and watched, sensing the weariness in her body, imagining he could see the tired droop of her shoulders even through the enveloping gown.

'All but done,' she murmured, and, perhaps sensing his presence, she turned.

Not that he could see much of her face. The combination of mask, protective glasses and cap all but covered it.

'We've mucked up the schedule, haven't we?' she said apologetically to him, and he wanted to go to her, take her in his arms, tell her schedules didn't matter and how much it hurt him to see her tired like this.

But Daniel, after delivering final advice to Sally, was walking towards him, which was just as well as Sally would probably have laughed at his urge to protect and cherish her.

Sally concentrated fiercely on the final stage of the operation. Behind her back she could hear Daniel explaining to Grant how they'd operated on the first climber but had thought this one was less severely injured.

'Then his intercranial pressure shot right up,' Daniel was saying. 'Fortunately, while Sally and I were grabbing a bite in the canteen before heading home.'

There was a murmur of another voice, Grant's voice, but she couldn't catch the words, so she securely taped the tube they'd left in place to drain any further fluid away and packed dressings around it to protect it.

Her mind drifted to Saturday night. To a kiss that had changed the balance between them, and had made it impossible to keep classifying what she felt as a one-sided attraction, and 'that night' as an aberration never to be repeated.

And better not remembered!

She'd have to face her boss some time, but the all-night operating session had given her a reprieve. Today, she was going home to catch up on some sleep.

CHAPTER ELEVEN

AND if Monday was a bad day, with delayed operations and overtime, Tuesday was worse. Complications in post-op patients forced a rethink of Wednesday's schedules when patients had to be readmitted to Theatre. Then Daniel called in to ask for compassionate leave. His wife had finally delivered an ultimatum to him and he needed time to try to fix his marriage.

By Friday, Sally was wondering why she'd taken on such a demanding specialty, thoughts of Grant and whatever lay between them a long way down the list of her worries. Getting some sleep came at the top, study came next, although even that no longer seemed so important.

True, her body still reacted to seeing Grant as they whisked in or out of the ward or passed in the theatre corridor, and especially during the student rounds when she had time to study his profile and muse on eyes as blue as the sky she rarely saw these days. But why this should be so, and whether anything would come of it, were questions she was too tired to consider.

Especially when she was sitting in her underwear, alone in the changing room, stripped of theatre gear, showered and dried, and now trying to summon up sufficient energy to pull on the rest of her clothes and drive home.

'Ha! At last I've found you. Hasn't it been a dreadful week? Are you OK? I know you've borne the brunt of it, and it will have thrown your study schedule all out.' Grant sat down beside her but, perhaps mindful of the fact that anyone could walk in, kept a good six inches between their bodies. 'Daniel should be back next week if you want a few days off yourself. Heaven knows, you deserve them.'

The words rushed at her, bringing with them a wave of dejection that the talk was all of work.

Which was how she really wanted things to be, she reminded herself, no longer listening to explanations of who could work what hours to allow her time off.

'Are you listening?' he demanded, and she turned to look at him, look into his eyes.

But what she saw there so confused her she looked away, which was when he reached out and drew her close, holding her tightly against his warm body, dropping kisses on her damp hair.

'I can't bear this,' he said. 'Can't bear seeing you working so hard, looking so tired, struggling to fit everything into your life.'

He spoke crossly, as if the dreadful week had been her fault.

'Well, don't blame me,' she muttered, and should have pulled away, but the warmth of his body was seeping into her cold one, and it made her feel...

Woozy?

She was trying to think of a better word to describe the comfort of it when he continued.

'It gives me a pain in the chest and I've made a fool of myself, going down to A and E for an ECG, where they found nothing at all wrong with my heart.'

The idea of him having an electrocardiogram was so preposterous Sally lifted her head off his shoulder and wriggled around so she could look at him again, but there was no hint of laughter in his blue eyes and his mouth looked grim.

Then as she watched, his lips moved, widening into a small, and somehow self-mocking, smile.

'But there is something wrong with my heart, Sally Cochrane. And you're to blame. Serves me right for getting involved with someone on the team.'

The admission, cryptic though it was, lifted some of Sally's weariness, enabling a couple of neurones to synapse.

'Was it because of Erica you made that stipulation? Did she hurt you so badly?'

She saw the frown pucker the skin between his dark eyebrows, and the blue eyes lose their shine.

Uh-oh. Wrong neurones!

'And who has been blabbing to you about Erica?'

Who? She didn't want to mention Paul or admit she'd listened to gossip.

'Tom mentioned something,' she said, aware it sounded lame.

'Oh, he did, did he?' Tom's brother muttered, then to Sally's astonishment he leant forward and kissed her gently on the lips.

'Erica is so far in the past she's nothing but an echo of a name,' he murmured, then he kissed her again. 'And it was something else that made me think…'

Sally was about to ask what something when he spoke again, and she guessed that subject was closed.

'It makes sense not to get involved, but did I take my own advice? Look at it from my viewpoint. I know the hours residents work, and how little time is left for study. To be distracting you from that, to kill your dreams of gaining your fellowship because I want to be with you—I can't be responsible for that, dear heart.'

She let him kiss her one more time—after all, it was very pleasant—before she asked the question.

'What makes you think I'd be so distracted?' She barely got the words out as the thought of no more kisses, just like that, made her want to cry.

'Wouldn't you be?' he murmured, tempting her lips again. 'I know I am. As well as needing an ECG, I've been wanting to take you off the operating schedule so you'll get some rest, and put my arm around you when you're looking tired, and carry you off to some quiet corner and kiss you at least a dozen times a day.'

'So what's the answer?' she demanded, totally confused by where this might be going. 'Do we pretend this never happened? Have one last smooch in the changing room and that's that?'

She thought for a minute then realised what she was feeling inside was no longer warm and woozy, but hot and angry.

'And why dump the onus on me? Why blame my dreams, my exams, my having to study, for not continuing to explore whatever it is between us?' She glared at him. Gold-flecked eyes indeed. What she needed was a couple of lasers to scorch right through him. 'It's an excuse, that's all, Grant Hudson. You were burnt once so now you don't want to take a risk. That's what all the talk of not getting involved within the team was about—self-protection for you. Well that's OK with me, because I like my men strong, not gutless.'

She grabbed her street clothes from the locker and pulled them on hurriedly, knowing the skirt was askew but not caring, then, while the cause of all her troubles sat silently on the bench, she stormed out of the room.

Given how closely their small team were forced to work together, it was surprising how little Sally saw of Grant during the following week. A two-day heads-of-department meeting helped, and scheduling that had her working nights later in the week also made a difference.

Although if he continued to do that—or to get Daniel who drew up the rosters to do it—she'd have to complai Working nights was usually better for studying, but as al' residents had study to do it wasn't fair she should be ' differently.

Late Saturday afternoon, she was in her study

from a good sleep and already stuck into the books. The gentle tap on the door was a new departure for her brothers, perhaps tired of being yelled at for interrupting her.

Grant stood there, looking doubtful, his hand still against the wooden jamb where he'd rapped his knuckles.

Only…

'Your brother said to go on in. Said you needed a distraction as you'd been working too hard.'

'Tom?'

The carbon copy nodded.

'Sam can do it, too,' he said. 'Uncanny, really, when friends we've known for years can't tell us apart.'

But Sally wasn't listening. She was on her feet, crossing the room heedless of the piles of books.

'Is something wrong? It wasn't a heart attack, was it? He's had pains in his chest. But he had an ECG—'

Tom caught her by the shoulders and squeezed his fingers reassuringly into her muscle.

'Hey! Calm down. There's nothing wrong.' Then he grinned and she saw similarities as well as differences. 'Apart from the fact that you ruined my honeymoon. I've been like a bear with a sore head, and poor Sam had the devil's own job getting me interested in anything.'

Sally shook her head.

'Either my brain's too numbed by study or you're not making much sense.'

He smiled again.

'It's a twin thing,' he explained, which didn't help at all. 'We've always had it. One of us gets hurt, the other one aches. One of us fell in love—'

'You're saying the only reason your brother felt anything for me was because he caught your love for Sam?' Sally threw up her arms in despair.

'Give me strength!' she muttered, and turned away from

him. Then, as he began to argue it wasn't what he'd meant, she remembered what he'd said earlier.

'Never mind that,' she said, waving away his explanation. 'How come *I've* ruined your honeymoon? Or is this another twin thing? Blaming someone else for every ill that befalls you?'

Tom sighed.

'I don't suppose I could have a cup of coffee?'

'No!' Sally snapped. 'At least, not until you've explained. Come in, shift the books off that chair and sit down.'

The second Dr Hudson did as he was told, then he sighed again, but finally, fixing blue eyes that were like, yet not like, others she fancied, began to talk.

'For a start, I should explain that Grant's got an over-developed responsibility gene. In our relationship I put it down to him being the first-born, but he carries it through to his work. When he had just been admitted as a fellow, and was appointed senior registrar, he had a fourth-year resident who fell madly in love with a second-year who came onto the team from another hospital.'

He glanced at Sally as if to check she was listening, but she guessed, from what she knew of Grant, he was marshalling his thoughts.

'It was a fairly torrid relationship from the start, and Grant was always worried about the effect it might have on both their work and study schedules. But when he spoke to his department head about it he was told it was their private business and not his concern.'

Sally felt a knot tightening in her stomach. She wasn't sure she needed to hear this story.

Yet she prompted him.

'So?'

Tom looked towards the window, then studied her bookshelves, before finally facing her again.

'It went on for eight months, the fourth-year failed his

finals. As you know, the names, on that final day, are put up on a list, and those who don't get through learn by omission. While those who passed went back into the college to be welcomed and inducted, he went back to the flat they shared, shot his girlfriend and hanged himself.'

There was a pause while the knot grew tighter and ice formed in Sally's blood.

'She didn't turn up for work and Grant went to look for her. He found the bodies, identified them for the police. He then took it on himself to clean up the flat. He won't talk about it—about any of it—but it has to have affected him.'

Sally closed her eyes and waited until the words had stopped hammering in her skull. She glanced at her watch.

'Where is he?'

Tom moved his head to indicate the apartment block.

'I'm on my way over to Toowong,' he said. 'But I thought you should know.'

She nodded, unable to find anything more to say. Certainly not 'thank you', although it did explain a lot.

Tom stood up, then came across and kissed her on the cheek.

'Good luck,' he said, as if he knew what she was going to do.

She listened to his footfalls down the hall and across the front verandah. Even imagined she could hear a car starting up in the street beyond the gate.

Then she stood up, carefully, like someone old and tired, and walked through to the bathroom where she washed her face and smoothed her hair down with damp fingers.

Still without a clue as to what she would say, she set out towards Grant's place. Under the railway bridge and up the hill, striding determinedly on, until she reached the foyer door.

Which was where she nearly turned tail and raced back home again. But her heart told her she had this one last chance, and her head told her if she didn't do it she'd be as cowardly as she'd labelled him.

She pressed the bell.

'It's Sally,' she said when he answered, although she knew he could see her on the screen.

He didn't reply but the front door lock snicked to tell her it was open and she walked in. Up in the lift, turn right. He was standing in the doorway, looking as tired and confused as she felt.

She went towards him, wanting only to put her arms around him and hold him close.

For ever.

But not yet, her head warned. Don't confuse things with sex!

So she walked past him, into the living room, and stood, looking out at the view.

'For as long as I can remember, being a doctor has been a dream. My dad used to tease me by telling people, "Sally's going to be a brain surgeon." And that idea took root as well.'

She turned and found he'd followed her so he was standing only a metre from her now. His expression was carefully neutral but his eyes were wary.

'I think now that I clung to it after he had died, because it was all I had. Something definite.' She shrugged with a kind of helplessness, finding the words hard to find, and even harder to say.

'You know how people tell you get a life. Well, perhaps if someone had come along, somewhere along the way— someone who'd meant a great deal to me—I'd have lost focus then, been diverted, gone into something easier, something that could accommodate a "life".'

He didn't move, said nothing, and she realised he wasn't going to help. That she was going to have to stammer her way through all of this without feedback or prompting.

'Anyway, that didn't happen, and I love the work, and I do want a career in neurosurgery, but...' She stalled, unable to go on because what came beyond that 'but' was new and scary.

'But?'

Finally he broke his silence—if only with one word.

'But I realise it's not enough. Not for me. I thought it would be, but I know now that it isn't.' She shrugged again and, feeling suddenly vulnerable, covered herself. 'I could make it that way again. If that's how life works out. But right now, I can't help feeling that there are more important things than stereotaxic operations and fibre-optic light sources.'

She looked into his eyes, and added, 'Things I'd be a fool not to at least investigate.'

He shook his head and came towards her, taking her in his arms and holding her tightly.

'You'd be a bigger fool to not finish your study, and you'd be disappointed in yourself if you didn't pass the exam and become a fellow.'

She nodded against his chest.

'We'll have to snatch our time together.'

She nodded again.

'I could work with you. Help you. Take you through old exam papers.'

He sounded so unlike himself, so uncertain somehow, that she freed herself a little and reached up on tiptoe to kiss him on the lips.

'And how much study would I get done?' she teased, a little breathlessly, when his response had convinced her he wasn't so uncertain after all.

'You'd study!' he growled, then he kissed her again. 'We could schedule the other stuff.'

'Tuesday night one hour of kisses, Thursday sex?'

Grant chuckled and led her across to the couch where they'd sat that fateful night.

'Are you sure about this, Sally? Certain you can handle an involvement at this crucial stage of your career?'

She snuggled against him, amazed by how good it felt to have someone worrying about her welfare.

'If I don't get in this year, I can do the exam again next year,' she assured him. 'Or in five years' time if we decide to have a family first and I want to stay home with the babies.'

She then realised just how far ahead her mind had leapt and sat back, her hand across her mouth to prevent further indiscretions.

Not that it worked

'I'm sorry! I'm rushing ahead. All you've talked about is a relationship. We barely know each other and I'm assuming—Not that it matters, I'd be happy to just have a relationship—'

He stopped the babble with a kiss and, when they stopped for breath, reassured her with words as well.

'The relationship I want with you is marriage, Sally Cochrane. Nothing less. But we'll do it properly, and take our time, and get to know each other first.'

Another kiss, more like a pledge this time.

'And I, too, can take time off to mind babies, but first we'll get you qualified so your dad's dream comes true.'

He kissed her again.

'Did I tell you I loved you?'

She smiled at him.

'Not yet.'

'Well, you haven't told me either,' he reminded her, and they kissed again and whispered all the words the kisses said but which they both needed to hear.

And on the verandah of the old house at Toowong Tom took his new bride in his arms and kissed the breath out of her.

'It's a twin thing,' he said, then he looked up to find her brothers watching. 'Just wait until it happens to you.'

MILLS & BOON®

Makes any time special™

Copyright © Harlequin Enterprises Limited 1997
All rights reserved

Mills & Boon publish 29 new titles every month. Select from...

Modern Romance™   Tender Romance™

Sensual Romance™

Medical Romance™   Historical Romance™

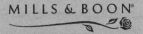

MILLS & BOON®

Medical Romance™

COMING HOME TO DANIEL by Josie Metcalfe

Denison Memorial Hospital

Believing that Daniel had died five years ago, Sam had comforted herself that at least she had his son to care for. But on returning home to take up a new locum position, she found Daniel alive and well—with a son only a few months older than their own!

DR MATHIESON'S DAUGHTER by Maggie Kingsley

Book two of St Stephen's Accident and Emergency duo

When Specialist Registrar and confirmed bachelor Dr Elliot Mathieson finds out he's a father, he begs his good friend, nurse Jane Halden for help. She can't refuse him, though maybe she should. Unknown to Elliot, Jane's been in love with him for years!

THE NURSE'S DILEMMA by Gill Sanderson

Book one of Nursing Sisters duo

Kate had always been a wanderer, but when she returned home, she found a reason to stay in Dr Steve Russell. However, he loved Kate because she wasn't looking for commitment and if she told him she loved him, she'd almost certainly lose him…

On sale 1st June 2001

Available at most branches of WH Smith, Tesco, Martins, Borders, Easons, Sainsbury, Woolworth and most good paperback bookshops 0501/03a

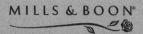

MILLS & BOON®

Medical Romance™

THE HONOURABLE DOCTOR by Carol Wood

Book one of Country Partners duo

Dr Marcus Granger and Dr Jane Court had been passionately in love, but she let Marcus marry her best friend, who was pregnant and terminally ill. Seven years later, widower Marcus is back. Can Jane ever forgive him for doing the honourable thing?

A HUSBAND TO TRUST by Judy Campbell

The day Mike Corrigan joined St Luke's as the new casualty doctor was the day that Sister Lindy Jenkins should have been married. Mike made it clear he was attracted to Lindy but if she risked her heart again, could he really be a husband to trust?

MIDWIFE UNDER FIRE! by Fiona McArthur

Midwife Noni Frost's maternity unit desperately needs to hire a new obstetrician, or it will be closed down. Obstetrician Iain McCloud tells her he is just a surgeon as he has reasons why he can't stay. But then he falls for Noni—how can he tell her the truth?

On sale 1st June 2001

Available at most branches of WH Smith, Tesco, Martins, Borders, Easons, Sainsbury, Woolworth and most good paperback bookshops

0501/03b

MILLS & BOON®

S&S/RTL3

MIRANDA LEE

Secrets & Sins

*Passion, sensuality and scandal
set amongst Australia's rich and famous*

A compelling six-part linked family saga.

Book 3 -Passion & The Past

Available from 1st June

*Available at branches of WH Smith, Tesco,
Martins, RS McCall, Forbuoys, Borders, Easons,
Volume One/James Thin and most good paperback bookshops*

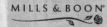
MILLS & BOON®

0501/114/MB13

IN HOT PURSUIT

Nat, Mark and Michael are three sexy men, each in pursuit of the woman they intend to have...at all costs!

Three brand-new stories for a red-hot summer read!

Vicki Lewis Thompson
Sherry Lewis
Roz Denny Fox

Published 18th May

Available at branches of WH Smith, Tesco, Martins, RS McCall, Forbuoys, Borders, Easons, Sainsbury, Woolworth and most good paperback bookshops

FREE!

4 Books
and a surprise gift!

We would like to take this opportunity to thank you for reading this Mills & Boon® book by offering you the chance to take FOUR more specially selected titles from the Medical Romance™ series absolutely FREE! We're also making this offer to introduce you to the benefits of the Reader Service™ —

     ★ FREE home delivery
     ★ FREE gifts and competitions
     ★ FREE monthly Newsletter
     ★ Books available before they're in the shops
     ★ Exclusive Reader Service discounts

Accepting these FREE books and gift places you under no obligation to buy; you may cancel at any time, even after receiving your free shipment. Simply complete your details below and return the entire page to the address below. *You don't even need a stamp!*

YES! Please send me 4 free Medical Romance books and a surprise gift. I understand that unless you hear from me, I will receive 6 superb new titles every month for just £2.49 each, postage and packing free. I am under no obligation to purchase any books and may cancel my subscription at any time. The free books and gift will be mine to keep in any case.

MIZEB

Ms/Mrs/Miss/Mr ....Initials................................
BLOCK CAPITALS PLEASE

Surname ....

Address..

....

....Postcode ....

Send this whole page to:
UK: The Reader Service, FREEPOST CN81, Croydon, CR9 3WZ
EIRE: The Reader Service, PO Box 4546, Kilcock, County Kildare (stamp required)

Offer not valid to current Reader Service subscribers to this series. We reserve the right to refuse an application and applicants must be aged 18 years or over. Only one application per household. Terms and prices subject to change without notice. Offer expires 30th November 2001. As a result of this application, you may receive further offers from Harlequin Mills & Boon Limited and other carefully selected companies. If you would prefer not to share in this opportunity please write to The Data Manager at the address above.

Mills & Boon® is a registered trademark owned by Harlequin Mills & Boon Limited.
Medical Romance™ is being used as a trademark.